Impact: A Riverdale PD Series Prequel

Riverdale PD Series

J.I. O'Neal

Published by River Walk Press, 2020.

This is a work of fiction. Similarities to real people, places, or events are entirely coincidental.

IMPACT: A RIVERDALE PD SERIES PREQUEL

First edition. March 31, 2020.

Copyright © 2020 J.I. O'Neal.

ISBN: 978-1393397175

Written by J.I. O'Neal.

Also by J.I. O'Neal

Riverdale PD Series
Impact: A Riverdale PD Series Prequel
Indiscriminate: 5th Anniversary Revised Edition
Time of Death

Stell-Ore War
The Crew of Cartage 15
Stell-Ore Justice

This book is dedicated to Ashley Davis-Holloway.

RIP

CHAPTER ONE

———

HIS LUNGS BURNED AS his breath heaved in ragged gasps. His feet pounded the wet pavement in short bursts before darting forward to cover the next expanse of sidewalk. He knew he had to stop or he might collapse. But if he did stop, the pain would come back – and he couldn't deal with that just now.

His cell phone rang. He ignored it through the first two rings, but by the third, he slowed to a jog and answered it. "Harkham," he said, out of breath.

"Noah? Everything okay?" Captain Ziehring asked.

Noah swallowed hard, gulping in air. "Yes, sir, just out for a run. Whatcha got?"

"I want you to come in to the station. There's something we need to discuss."

Noah's stomach clenched. Walking now, he found himself nearing one of Riverdale's major sources of income: the dockyard. He'd run almost six miles. "What is it? Do I have a case?"

"I'd rather not get into it over the phone. See you in, say, an hour?" The Captain's voice sounded strained. Seems he wasn't looking forward to their meeting, and Noah was starting to feel the same way.

"Yes, sir, I'll be there."

"Good. See you then." Ziehring hung up.

Noah walked for a few minutes back the way he had come, giving his body a chance to cool down before he waved down a cab and directed the driver to drop him at his apartment.

───────────

THIRTY MINUTES LATER, having showered and changed into a suit, Noah stepped off the bus a block away from the Fifth Precinct. He found Ziehring in his office. Across from the captain's old oak desk sat a man Noah didn't recognize, though he could only see him in slight profile. He looked a few years older than Noah, somewhere in his mid- to late-thirties, average build, roughly six-foot-two with dark blonde hair conservatively cut. He wore a grey suit – nothing too expensive, just tasteful and conventional.

Noah knocked on the captain's door, and entered the room at Ziehring's gesture. Ziehring stood, unfolding his tall, lean frame and smoothing his navy tie. He motioned one hand toward Noah. "This is Detective Sergeant Noah Harkham, the one I was telling you about," Ziehring said.

The man now turned in his chair and regarded Noah with a friendly expression. He looked more like an English teacher, Noah thought; the kind the guys might think was a little bit cool and the girls would have a crush on. His bearing, however, revealed that he, too, was a cop.

The man stood and extended his hand. "Detective Alan Franks. I've heard a lot about you."

Noah noticed his accent was unusually flat, which made it hard to pinpoint what part of the country he might be from. He wasn't a Midwesterner...at least not from Indiana like Noah. He shook the detective's hand, but shot an inquisitive look at his captain.

Ziehring ran a hand over his thin red hair and put his other hand on Noah's back. "Have a seat, Noah," he said, gesturing to a second chair as he returned to his own. "Noah," he said, his green eyes and lean face looking serious, "no one here understands how hard the last few months have been for you more than I do. But I feel – and I think Meares would agree with me – that it's time for you to move on." Ziehring flicked a glance at Franks. "Detective Franks has just transferred in from Atlanta. He's going to be your new partner."

Franks had apparently been briefed on Noah's situation; he was watching him with a sympathetic half-smile. There was a writhing in Noah's gut. Three months Rob Meares had been dead and already Ziehring expected him to just accept some stranger in his place?

Noah looked at each of them, got up, and walked out without a word.

Halfway down the hallway, he stopped short, running his fingers across the back of his neck and fighting against the knot that constricted his heart. He paced a ten-by-ten section of the hallway, trying to control his breathing. His thoughts raced from accusing himself of betraying Rob by not telling Ziehring right away that he didn't want a new partner to reminding himself that Franks was not to blame and that he should just give the guy a chance, to reprimanding himself for acting so childish by walking out. *What am I supposed to do?*

Not for the first time he wished Rob were here, that his mentor hadn't been taken from him so soon. He could almost hear Rob's voice now. "Get yer backside off the ground and yer head in the game." Noah smiled, in spite of himself, and turned back toward his captain's office only to see Franks walking toward him. He groaned but held his ground until the detective reached him.

"Obviously, this isn't going to be comfortable for either of us," Franks said without preamble. "I already feel like an intruder just coming into this precinct, let alone this...position. If you want me to talk to Ziehring about partnering me with someone else, just say the word."

Noah lifted one eyebrow. "You don't have to worry about me doing my job, Franks. I'm not broken."

"I didn't say –"

"I wasn't finished," Noah said. "I don't like the idea of you as my partner, okay? But whether we like each other or not doesn't even factor into it. The bottom line is that there's a job to be done, so just... don't get in my way."

Franks just nodded. "We've got a hit-and-run case near someplace called James Park. Unis just called it in, and the captain wants us on it." He peered at Noah, as if assessing his reaction.

Noah took a breath. Time to focus. "That's a suburb just east of the city. Come on," he said, "we'll need to requisition a car." He turned and headed down the tiled hallway toward the parking lot where unmarked cars were kept.

Franks called after him. "I have a car. I can drive, if you tell me where we're going."

Noah paused. Even after living here all these years, he had to admit he still hated driving in the city. It was the main reason he didn't own a car. "Fine," he conceded. "I'll get my kit."

CHAPTER TWO

———

AS THEY LEFT THE CITY behind, the early spring sky opened up, drenching the already soaked land and darkening Noah's already sour mood. Franks was a good driver, though – especially for not being familiar with the area – and followed Noah's directions without incident. Beyond that, no words passed between them.

They arrived on scene a little after 4:30, about ten minutes after the rain. Noah led the way, his crime scene kit in hand. Uniformed officers had the street blocked off with their cruisers and police tape. They had erected some screens as well, blocking the scene from direct view. The medical examiner's van was just a few feet away.

Neighbors and witnesses stood in huddled groups on nearby porches, crying and trying to comfort one another. Noah glanced toward the body lying in the road. It was very small: a child.

"Damn," he muttered as he and Franks approached the tape line.

"Oh, no," Franks muttered, "she's just a kid."

"Yeah," Noah replied, "but I meant the rain. It's gonna make processing the scene nearly impossible." He ignored the puzzled, almost offended look on Franks' face and continued on past the perimeter.

A pair of officers held a couple of umbrellas over the little girl's body and Dr. Lee, the medical examiner, knelt at her side, clad in a Tyvek suit and gloves. He examined the young girl's neck with gentle, efficient strokes. "Afternoon, Noah," Dr. Lee drawled amiably, squinting his warm brown eyes against the rain.

"Afternoon, Marvin," he replied, giving the genteel doctor a respectful nod. "The umbrellas your idea?"

"Yes, sirree. I know how grumpy you get when your scene is compromised," Lee answered.

Noah grunted. "I'm not grumpy. I just don't like it when things make my job harder. Speaking of which..." he added, looking around. He spotted Franks, deep in conversation with one of the uniformed officers and motioned him over. "Dr. Marvin Lee, our medical examiner," Noah said when Franks arrived, "this is Detective Franks, in from Atlanta."

"Nice to meet you," Franks said, with a nod of his head.

"At least you didn't try to shake my hand," Lee bantered, his careworn face crinkling in a smile as he rubbed his blood-smeared gloved hands together. "So you visitin' or do you plan to stay?"

"I'm here as long as they'll have me," he said with a sideways glance at Noah. "Harkham, the first responder says we have a witness, of a sort."

"'Of a sort?'"

Franks shrugged and gestured toward a man standing under the nearest porch, his arms wrapped around his thin frame. He was balding, somewhat short and wore wire-rimmed glasses and a long brown cardigan over a blue button-down shirt and tan pants.

"The girl –Tasha Bailey, eleven years old – was on her way home from a friend's house. That's them over there: the Reynoldses," he added with a nod to a family of four that stood with the witness. "Our guy's name is Oliver Crandall; he lives next door. Says he heard the girl scream and then the impact, but by the time he got outside, the car was 'taking off like a rabbit scenting a hound.' His words, according to the officer."

"You got all that in the two minutes you talked to the first responder?"

Franks dipped his head. "I'm easy to talk to."

"Right. All finished here, Doc? The rain's not doing us any favors and I'd like to start processing her as quickly as possible."

Dr. Lee stood. "She's all yours. We know time and mode of death, and I'd say the cause is a rather nasty skull fracture, though massive internal injuries will be a close contender. Poor lamb didn't have a chance." He stepped away, back near the tapeline while the detectives took over.

Noah gazed at the small, still form and sighed. Franks was right: it was always bad when it was a kid. She wore a red raincoat over a pair of pink and white tights and a denim skirt. A portion of her white cotton blouse peeked out from under the raincoat. Long glossy black curls obscured her face. One hand lay on the asphalt, pale as milk. She looked so still and perfect.

Noah knelt near her and retrieved two pairs of nitrile gloves from his kit. "Help me turn her," he instructed, handing Franks the second pair.

Franks slipped in beside one of the two officers holding the umbrellas, positioning himself at the girl's head. He slid his hands under her slim shoulders while Noah took hold of her legs. "Easy now," Noah directed, "lift up then flip. Don't let her scrape the road." He waited until Franks nodded. "Okay, on three. One – two – three."

Her hair swept aside as they turned her, revealing slightly open, rich brown eyes and a pale, heart-shaped face. Despite the damage the car had done, he could see she would have been pretty when she grew up. He tore his gaze from her little face and began scanning her clothing with a discerning eye, not touching it unless absolutely necessary. "Here we go," he said after a few moments.

"What is it?" Franks asked.

Noah pointed to the flat metal buttons on her coat. They were scratched up and held streaks and specks of gold-colored paint. "Transfer. I can't say for certain until the lab guys do their thing, but I'm positive that'll be paint from the car that hit her. Did your witness say what kind of car he saw?"

"I was about to go talk to him before you called me over," he replied. "I can go do that now, if you'd like."

Noah nodded, and Franks left. Noah used a scalpel and small vial to collect the paint samples, but after about five minutes, concluded there wouldn't be much more physical evidence on the girl. He stood, grabbed his kit and made a slow circle around her, sweeping a critical gaze over the pavement. Her body lay in the middle of a set of long, stuttering skid marks. After photographing and taking samples from the tire marks, he widened his spiraling orbit around her.

It was on his fourth revolution when he saw it: a small linear streak of reddish-brown fluid that was already dissolving in the falling rain. He dipped a cotton swab in the fluid and brought it to his nose. It smelled a little like burnt syrup. Brake fluid. He photographed and sampled the liquid to have the lab analyze it further.

That explained why it looked like whoever hit her had tried to stop, but wasn't able to completely until after he was already past her body. The brakes would have been slow to respond as fluid leaked out. He eyed the stop sign down the road and walked to it. As expected, there was the remnant of a larger streak of brake fluid.

Noah photographed this new puddle and took more samples. Unfortunately, he couldn't tell from the stain which way the car had gone from there, but, given the amount of fluid on scene, it wouldn't have gone far before the brakes failed altogether. Noah finished collecting everything he could find and walked back to meet up with Dr. Lee.

"I'm through here, Doc," Noah told Dr. Lee. "You can take her now." He peeled off his gloves and shoved them into his kit's waste bag. He gave the girl one last look, swiping rainwater off his face and hair. Noah didn't pray anymore, but he still hoped she was being taken care of in Heaven now that her earthly suffering was ended.

Dr. Lee gestured to his assistant, some wet-behind-the-ears intern barely out of his teens, to bring the gurney. The two, aided by the umbrella guard, stowed her away in a body bag and wheeled her toward the coroner's office van. They were putting her into the back when a blue SUV came screeching to a halt just outside the perimeter. A man and a woman, both dark-haired, exited the vehicle in a panic.

"Tasha!" The woman screamed through falling tears. She stopped short, trembling head to toe, at the sight of the body bag. Noah got to her just as her knees buckled, catching her before she collapsed to the ground.

"No, no, my baby," she cried, hitting his shoulders and chest.

"I'm sorry," he muttered to her, supporting her while she screamed and cried. He felt tears sting the backs of his own eyes and closed them for a moment. He then looked past her to the man, who stood stock still and pale, staring in disbelief. The Reynolds couple rushed toward him and the trio embraced. Mrs. Reynolds broke free a moment later and relieved Noah of the girl's mother.

She smiled at him with wet, reddened eyes. "I've got her now, Detective," she assured him, "thank you."

"Take them inside where it's dry. They shouldn't be here for this," he told her.

He turned to look at the Reynolds children, a young man of about eighteen or so and a girl who looked eleven or twelve, about the same age as the victim. The girl was seated on the bench by the front door, sobbing uncontrollably while her brother sat with his arm around her, his face a mask of shock. "We're going to do everything we can to find who did this," he told the two women next to him. "I promise." His voice was thick with emotion.

Mrs. Reynolds blinked free a tear. "Thank you," she said, steering the grieving mother toward the house. He watched them go, taking a moment to run the back of his hand across his wet eyes, mentally berating himself for not maintaining his professionalism and for making a promise he wasn't guaranteed to keep. He knew better than that.

He picked up his kit and put it in Franks' silver Chrysler before joining him on the porch. Franks adjusted his posture to include Noah in the conversation. "This is Detective Sergeant Harkham," he told Mr. Crandall, "he'll be working primary on this case. Do you mind telling him what you just told me?"

Mr. Crandall nodded and took a deep breath. "All I can remember is that the car was like a tan or goldish color and it had a lavender-purple stripe down the side." Noah could tell from his accent that he was a local. "Older, maybe from the late nineties or so. I think it was just the one guy in it, but I can't be a hundred percent on that." His arms still hugged his body and he shifted his weight from one foot to the other repeatedly.

Noah glanced at the blue hybrid parked along the curb. "Is that your car there, Mr. Crandall?"

He nodded. "Yes, sir."

"And the Reynoldses, what kind of car do they drive?"

Mr. Crandall furrowed his brow. "They have that white truck in the driveway there and she – Mrs. Reynolds, that is – drives the red SUV. It'll be in the garage, I expect. I've seen the boy driving both of 'em, so I don't think he's got his own. But I don't see what that has to do with anything."

"We just need to account for every vehicle we can, Mr. Crandall. Now, I need you to think back over the last few weeks for me. Do you remember seeing the car that hit Tasha before today?"

Mr. Crandall closed his eyes. After a moment he shook his head and looked at the two detectives. "No, don't believe so. Ugly as it was, I would have remembered."

"Okay," Noah said. He smiled. "That's good. Now, and I apologize for making you go through this again, can you remember hearing the tires squeal?"

Mr. Crandall swallowed hard, his eyes misting. "Yeah. I heard them."

"Before or after the scream?"

"Uh...before," he wiped away a tear that fell down his face. His face scrunched in concentration. "And after." He looked at Noah, working it out in his head. "Yeah, both before and after, like he slammed on the brakes, hit her, but didn't stop until after."

"Okay. And when you came outside, the car was where?"

Mr. Crandall pointed to the place just beyond the last set of skid marks, where Noah had found the brake fluid. "There. It was speeding off like a coon with a hound on his tail."

Noah tried not to smile at the very Southern simile. "Okay, thank you very much. If you would just make sure you give your contact details to the officer over there, we'd very much appreciate it." Noah took one of his business cards out of his pocket and handed it to Mr. Crandall. "If you think of anything else or need to get in touch with us, just call me at this number. All right?"

Mr. Crandall took the card and nodded. "All right."

Noah looked at Franks. "Okay, let's go talk to the family."

Franks took a breath. "After you," he said.

Noah shared his dread – this was always the hardest part of any homicide investigation. Noah started into the house.

That's when they heard the yelling.

CHAPTER THREE

───

NOAH RUSHED INTO THE Reynolds' house, gun drawn. Franks was one step behind. They cleared the entry and formal sitting room then followed the sounds of commotion to the family room toward the back of the house. Noah and Franks cautiously peered around the doorframe into the room.

Noah returned his gun to its holster, motioning for Franks to do the same. The young Reynolds girl was on the floor. Her body shuddered and jerked in some sort of seizure, and her parents knelt next to her, buffering her throes to keep her from hurting herself. They called her name and spoke in comforting tones. The brother sat on the couch, bare feet drawn up into the seat, hugging his knees to his chest. The Baileys stood huddled together across the room, near the stone fireplace, staring in shock and concern.

Franks slipped past Noah and took off his suit jacket, folded it and placed it under the girl's head. Noah used his radio to call it in. "Dispatch, this is 2259 requesting an ambulance at our location. We've got a young girl having a seizure."

"Copy that, 2259," replied Noah's favorite dispatcher, Joyce Collins. "Ambulance en route, ETA...six minutes."

Noah approached the family and knelt beside Mrs. Reynolds. "I've called for an ambulance. They're on their way. How can we help in the meantime?"

Mr. Reynolds looked up, his face surprisingly calm. "She has epilepsy. The stress... we just need to ride it out. She'll be fine."

"If it's all the same, I would still like the paramedics to check her over, just to be sure," Noah replied.

Mr. Reynolds regarded him a moment, his lean, pleasant-looking face drawn and weary. "Thank you, Detective." He turned his attention to Franks, who still sat at the girl's head. "Both of you. Thank you."

Franks smiled at him. "I have a cousin who has epilepsy. It's tough, but he's got it under control now. She'll be fine."

Noah went over to the Bailey couple and laid a hand on Mrs. Bailey's arm. "Why don't we go into the kitchen?"

The two moved away at his direction, tearing their gazes from the girl on the floor. Once in the Reynolds' quaint and neat kitchen, the couple seemed to sag under the weight of the tragic events. They seated themselves at the island bar, leaving Noah to face them from across the counter.

"I want to start by saying how very sorry I am that this has happened to your family," he told them. "I can't imagine how you must be feeling, but I promise that my partner and I will do everything we can to find who is responsible." He had hesitated on the word partner and hoped the couple hadn't noticed. It was important to present himself and Franks as a cohesive unit dedicated to getting justice for their daughter, no matter what he may think of the man personally.

Mrs. Bailey sobbed quietly. She buried her face in her hands, the sleeves of her gauzy blouse pulled up over her palms to hide her tears. Noah had only seen her face full on for a few moments, but he could see that little Tasha favored her mother more than her father, who was lighter of hair and eye and squarer of face. Mr. Bailey swallowed a time or two, then nodded as tears ran down his face. He rubbed his wife's back and rested his chin on her head, murmuring to her.

Noah shifted his weight. "I apologize, but I have to ask you a couple of questions, if you feel up to it."

Mr. Bailey turned his gaze to Noah, but then nodded. "Okay. Were you both aware that Tasha was here today?"

"Yes," Mr. Bailey said. "She spends part of almost every day with Natalie. They've been best friends since birth, practically. We only live a couple streets over."

"Natalie? That's the Reynolds girl?" Mr. Bailey nodded, so Noah continued. "Have either of you noticed any tan or light gold colored vehicles in the neighborhood? Anyone you don't recognize parked in the area, anything like that?"

"No. I haven't," Mr. Bailey replied.

Mrs. Bailey looked up. "Are you saying someone did this on purpose?"

"I'm not saying anything, Mrs. Bailey," Noah assured her. "I'm just trying to follow up on every possibility. But, if it were... premeditated, can either of you think of anyone who might want to harm your family?"

They both went stiff. "Who would want to hurt our little girl?" Mrs. Bailey demanded. "What kind of people do you think we are that someone would – would do this just to get to us? We're just...I don't know, normal people!"

Mr. Bailey shushed her, holding her close. "We're not important enough for anything like that, Detective Harkham. My wife is a realtor and I work in an office. My company sells office supplies. We've never done anything to anyone to warrant this kind of retaliation."

Noah already knew from this first year of experience as a detective that there were many, many reasons that had nothing to do with status or importance a person might seek vengeance against someone else. He let the subject drop, however; nothing so far suggested Tasha's death was premeditated.

"All right. We'll let you know as soon as we have anything concrete." He withdrew one of his cards from his jacket pocket and laid it on the countertop in front of the grieving couple.

"In the meantime, call me any time – any time – if you need anything at all."

"Thank you, Detective Harkham" Mr. Bailey said.

Noah nodded. He slipped from the room, letting the couple grieve in privacy. When he returned to the living room, Natalie Reynolds was alert and sitting up with her father's support. Franks had retrieved his jacket, which was now draped over his arm, but stood nearby as if he feared a relapse. Mrs. Reynolds held her daughter's hand, speaking calmly to her.

Noah gestured for Franks to follow him out to the now-empty porch. "Is she ok?" Noah asked him once they were outside.

Franks gave an ambiguous dip of his head. "It seems to have passed for now. I wouldn't be surprised if it happens again a few more times in the coming weeks. My cousin's attacks would always get worse if he was under a lot of stress."

Noah accepted this in silence. He moved to the sidewalk as he heard the ambulance's sirens signaling its approach. The ambulance pulled up to the perimeter of the crime scene and two paramedics exited: a cute, petite blonde woman and an older, stocky guy.

"We were just here, Harkham," the woman said, "And we checked everyone over before we left."

"What happened?" her partner asked as they got to the edge of the Reynolds' property. "Dispatch said a child is having a seizure."

"The Reynolds girl is epileptic," Franks informed them. "She's come out of it now, but we thought you ought to take a look."

They nodded and hurried past the two detectives. Noah started to walk away. "Shouldn't we stay until the paramedics are finished?" Franks asked.

Noah shook his head. "We have evidence we need to get processed. There's nothing we can do for anyone here."

Franks nodded, following Noah back toward the car. "Is this how a homicide always is? I mean, witnessing the worst moments of people's lives, offering whatever trite words we can then just leaving them to their grief?"

Noah regarded his partner a moment. "What division were you in before you came here?"

Franks looked a bit uncomfortable. "I was in Central Investigations. We mostly handled robberies and fraud."

"Major Crimes is a whole different world," Noah answered. "Especially a homicide. We just need to follow the evidence, that's the only way we can help them now." With that, he got into the car.

Franks got in a moment later. He started the car, but turned to Noah. "I'm not a rookie. I just want you to know that. I've seen bodies before; I just never handled the investigations myself."

Noah furrowed his brow. "Most of our cops come into Major Crimes from different backgrounds. You don't owe me any kind of explanation. Just because you don't come from Homicide doesn't mean you won't be a good homicide detective."

Franks peered at him as if assessing his sincerity. "Thank you," he said.

"But if you were a screw-up in Atlanta and got shipped to me so they could get rid of you, I need to know that now."

Franks looked stunned and offended. "I asked to come here."

"Why?"

"That's none of your business."

"It is if you want to be my partner. No secrets. No lies. I have to know I can trust you with my life and vice versa."

Franks took a deep breath. "My mother lives here. She's ill. Dying, actually. I came here to be close by until she... until the end."

Noah went still, then rubbed his hand across the back of his neck. "I'm sorry."

Franks shrugged. "No, it's okay. You're right, no secrets and no lies."

"Okay, then: what's with that accent?"

Noah was surprised to see Franks smile. "I knew that was bothering you." He put the car in gear and drove away from the scene. "I took voice lessons, like the kind a lot of news anchors take."

"Okay. Why?"

Franks grinned at him and spoke in a slow drawl. "I come from Alabama. I never wanted to stay down south for the rest of my life and I knew I wanted to be a cop. I didn't want to be seen as 'some dumb southern hick cop' by you Yanks, so I took lessons to flatten the south right out of mouth, so to speak."

Noah stared at him a long moment. "You're serious right now?"

Franks laughed. "Yes, I'm serious," he said in his 'normal' accent. "I've seen how people judge each other on the most superficial things. I didn't want anything to hinder my chances of joining a more northern precinct and I don't want anyone to think I'm stupid just because I didn't talk like a northerner."

"Riverdale isn't exactly northern. Neither was Atlanta."

Franks gave a conceding tilt of his head. "True. But I haven't decided I'm staying here the rest of my life either."

"So you're saying I shouldn't try to get used to you being here. Next stop New York, then?"

Franks ignored this question and asked one of his own. "So what about you? You're obviously not from around here, what's your story?"

Noah hesitated. "I moved here from Indiana when I was sixteen."

"Wow. What brought you that far from home?"

Noah turned to the window. "My parents were murdered."

CHAPTER FOUR

———

FRANKS PULLED INTO the parking lot of the Calera County Crime Lab and sneaked another look at his new partner. Noah Harkham was a bit of a puzzle. He looked a little like Superman – square of jaw, dark of hair, though his eyes were the color of smoked-glass instead of blue – but he had none of the boyish charm associated with the iconic superhero's alter-ego. Noah wasn't exactly cold, but Franks definitely did not feel welcomed.

He knew much of that lay in the fact that Noah's partner – his first partner and mentor, according to Captain Ziehring – had been dead barely three months and now the case that he and Noah had been working had gone cold. Trying to acclimate to a new partner could be stressful under normal circumstances, and Noah's circumstances were anything but normal.

Franks couldn't help but wonder if the fact that Noah was an orphan also played into his cool demeanor. Losing both parents – to murder, nonetheless – was bound to mess you up and he guessed Noah was just trying to protect himself from further hurt by not getting close to anyone else.

Or maybe he just doesn't like me... They got out of the car and Franks got his first glimpse of the crime lab. He wasn't very impressed. It was a modest, three-story brick building that looked like an old factory of some sort. The windows were newer and sleeker, with black metal frames and sepia-tinted glass. The door they entered by was of the same style and bore the establishment's name in stark white lettering. The floor was cream-colored tile and the walls of the foyer and lobby were a dark dusty blue. The ceilings were high and the large windows of the façade let in enough natural light to avoid feeling closed in.

Noah veered away from the reception area, where a dark-haired woman of slim build sat behind a desk of dark granite atop cream painted wood. She flashed a smile in Noah's direction, eyed Franks a moment, then dismissed the pair of them from her attention altogether. Franks continued to follow Noah to the right of the lobby where a stainless steel L-shaped stairway led up to the next floor. A security guard watched them approach, but only nodded to Noah and let them pass.

"So," Franks whispered to Noah as they mounted the stairs, "I take it you come here often?" He smiled at his own lame joke as Noah gave him a sidelong glance.

"Yeah, I have a degree in forensics, and, as you can see, our lab is pretty small, so I process my own scenes and deliver the evidence to the techs. We have criminalists who act as crime scene unit officers and as lab technicians, but they get stretched pretty thin sometimes and this way saves time for everyone."

Franks decided to take advantage of Noah's apparent willingness to play tour guide. "How many people work here?"

"Right now we have two shifts – day and night. Each shift has three to four criminalists. We also have about twenty techs who only work in the lab. Then there's security and administrative personnel." They reached the second floor landing and were faced with a hallway running to their right and another leading straight ahead, back toward the front of the building.

"This way," Noah said, indicating the passage straight ahead.

The floors here were covered in neutral high-traffic carpet and the walls were the same cream as the reception desk downstairs. Somebody got a good deal on that color.

The hallway terminated in a glass-walled lounge, which was now occupied by about half a dozen people in lab coats. To their right, another hallway continued past small labs and rooms whose sole purpose seemed to be to house one long lab table and not much else. Some of these rooms had technicians working in them, others stood dark and unused. Noah led the way to an intersecting hallway and turned left. He stopped at a lab where a tall, young guy with bleach-blonde hair sat on a stool, peering into a dissecting scope.

Noah rapped his knuckles on the door frame and the man looked up. "Hey, Noah! What's up?" The man's voice was warm and his accent sounded very west coast. Franks noticed a slight resemblance to a young Henry Fonda, an actor he liked very much. "Who's our new friend?"

"Detective Alan Franks," Noah said. "Franks, this is Conrad Ward, one of our criminalists."

Franks gave a small wave. "Hello."

Conrad tipped two fingers out from his brow in return. "Nice to meet ya. What brings you guys in?" He eyed the evidence bags in Noah's hand.

"We got a hit-and-run. I've got paint samples and what I'm pretty sure is brake fluid. But, of course, I'll let you tell me," he added with a grin.

"Hit-and-run, huh? Anyone hurt?" Conrad asked, taking the evidence bags from Noah and signing the chain of custody form on each.

"A little girl," Franks answered. "It's a vehicle versus pedestrian incident. Fatal."

Conrad looked up sharply. "Ah, crap, that sucks. How young?"

"Eleven," Noah answered.

Conrad shook his head. "That's awful. Well, I'm your man, so let me log this in and I'll start getting it processed."

"You'll call the minute you have anything?"

"Of course," Conrad answered. His expression grew concerned. "So, uh, how ya been, Harkham? I haven't seen you around much lately, since..."

Noah's jaw clenched. "I'm fine," he said through gritted teeth. Then his expression softened a little. "Really, I'm doing okay. Thanks, Conrad. Just, uh, give me a call when you're done with those."

"Yeah, definitely. Take care, man."

Noah gave him a half-hearted smile and brushed past Franks out the door. "So, Franks," Conrad said as Franks turned to follow Noah, "will we be seeing you around?"

"Yeah, I'll be around." He glanced at his partner, who was just about to the intersecting corridor, and added, "If Harkham doesn't run me out of town first."

Conrad snorted. "Don't mind him, he's more bark than bite...for the most part."

Franks gave Conrad a parting nod and followed Noah. For the most part... Great.

CHAPTER FIVE

THE FIRST DAY ENDED...well, it kind of just ended. Franks expected some awkward moment as the day wrapped up, but it went better than he could have hoped. Of course, that was probably because Noah had gone back to ignoring him and Franks was left to fill out his reports on his own. Noah had updated him on the results of the canvass he'd ordered the uniformed officers to complete, however, so he hadn't been forgotten entirely.

The update hadn't been good. No one else had seen or heard anything for six blocks in all directions from the scene and so the trail of the killer's vehicle was lost. Noah was looking into getting footage from local businesses' surveillance cameras and traffic cameras around the neighborhood, which left Franks with little more to do than get acquainted with his new precinct.

By the time Ziehring came to tell him he should call it a day, Franks had lost track of where Noah even was, so he just left. He got back to his hotel room around nine that evening, changed into a tee shirt and flannel pants and settled in to veg in front of the television. He ordered a pizza and found a movie, *The Third Man*, to while away the few hours before hitting the sack. He was about forty-five minutes into the film when his cell phone rang. Franks looked at the caller ID and frowned.

"Hello?"

"We've got a lead on the car. Where are you?"

"Harkham?" Franks sat up and turned off the television.

"Yes. Where are you, I'll pick you up."

Franks pulled off his flannel pants and looked around for the pants he'd worn that day. "Um, I'm at my hotel room. It's the Marriott on College Avenue."

"Okay, I can be there in fifteen minutes." Franks heard a car horn honking. Noah sighed. "Make that twenty; I'm stuck in a slight traffic jam."

Franks laughed. "Just flip on your siren, that oughtta clear things up."

"Don't tempt me," Noah replied. "Be ready, I don't want to waste time coming up to get you, we need to jump on this thing now."

Franks zipped up his pants and stripped his tee shirt off. "No problem. I'll be in the parking lot."

"Good," Noah said, just before hanging up.

Franks hung up. "Okay, bye," he said sarcastically. He finished getting dressed and walked down to the parking lot. The rain had stopped a few hours earlier, but now he felt a few misty drops hit his face and hands as he stood waiting. Just as Noah pulled up in the unmarked cruiser, the sky opened up again, drenching Franks in the few seconds it took him to slide into the passenger seat.

He ran his hand over his hair, flicking off water onto the floorboards. "Temperature's dropped," he remarked with a shiver.

Noah leaned forward and turned the heat on low. "Be glad it's not any later in the year. It just gets unbearably humid on rainy days here in the summer."

"So you said we have a lead on the car?" Franks asked as he and Noah drove back toward the highway that would take them to James Park.

"Yeah. Got a call from the owner of the gas station about a block from the Reynolds' house. He found the car dumped behind his building. A patrol car is there now to keep it locked down for us."

Franks furrowed his brow. "How did the canvassing officers miss it?"

Noah grunted. "I don't know, but I'd like to find out. We've lost hours because of this."

Franks hoped that some poor unlucky SOB didn't get reamed for this mistake, but he thought it highly likely. Noah didn't seem to be very tolerant of...inefficiency, to say the least. He left the broody detective to his thoughts and turned his own to his mother's health. The doctors had given her a little less than six months to live, unless they could find her a new heart.

But, since she was over sixty-five, the likelihood of that happening was pretty much slim to none. He hadn't been to church since he was a child, but Franks hoped God would offer up some kind of miracle. Grown man or not, he still couldn't imagine his life without his mother. Especially after losing his father just three years ago. His stomach felt cold and twisted up every time he thought about it.

He risked a sidelong glance at his new partner. He couldn't imagine what it must've been like for Noah to lose both his parents at such a young age. Of course he wanted to know more about what had happened to them and how Noah had dealt with the loss, but he was the last person Noah would want to discuss the topic with right now.

The ride out to the suburb seemed to go by more quickly this time, and before long, they had pulled up to the Gulp 'n Guzzle on Hyacinth Drive. A patrol car was parked just to the side of the building in the gravel, its lights scattering like handfuls of rubies and sapphires tossed out in the rain. They got out of the car and approached the officer standing watch over the abandoned vehicle.

Franks was instantly sure they had the right car: it was a 1998 Pontiac Bonneville with metallic gold paint and a purple stripe all down the side. "Vikings colors," he said, referring to the football team.

Noah nodded. "This has to be our murder weapon."

"The call came in about thirty minutes ago, Detectives," the officer – one T. Kendall, according to his nametag – said as soon as they were within earshot. "I haven't touched anything, but visual inspection shows it's empty, except for the beer bottles and drug paraphernalia all over the place."

"Perfect," Noah said with a glance into the car's interior. "We should be able to get DNA and prints galore in there." He gestured for the officer to pop the lock on the passenger side door and stepped out of his way. As soon as the door was open, Noah pulled on some nitrile gloves and opened the glove compartment. A moment later, he made a small sound of triumph. "Franks," he called.

Franks stepped closer and peered over Noah's back to the registration he held in his hand. "Who are we looking for?"

"Registration's outdated, but it says this car belongs to a Carmen Meeks. The address is in Pond Hollow."

"What is that, another neighborhood like this one?"

The officer snorted a laugh. Noah shot him a look. "Um, no. That's the really skeevy trailer court at the edge of town we passed on the way here."

"Ah."

"It's a known hangout for prostitutes and drug dealers," Kendall added.

"Yeah, I got that," Franks said.

Noah bagged the registration and shut the door. He walked to the front and shone a small flashlight across the hood. "There are scratches on the hood. Faint, but definitely there. This has to be it." He shone his light at Kendall. "Get this thing towed back to the lab. I want Parker on this immediately. Tell him Ward has the samples from the victim so he can compare it to the car's paint. Tell him to check the brake lines, too."

Kendall hopped to, getting on his radio and calling for a tow truck. Noah led the way back to the car. "C'mon," he said over his shoulder, "with any luck we'll catch Ms. Meeks at home."

Noah pulled up to Lot #12 about ten minutes later. The lights were on, which Franks took to be a good sign, but no one answered when they knocked on the aluminum framed storm door. Noah tried the handle and found it unlocked, so he opened the outer door and pounded his fist on the wooden inner door. A moment later they heard a heavy thud followed by a loud and very unladylike expletive.

"Keep yer pants on!" a woman yelled. Heavy footsteps approached the door. "At least til ya want me t'take 'em off y-" she stopped short as she jerked the door open and found the two men on her doorstep. She was in her mid-forties, with lank dishwater brown hair and faded blue eyes. She was clad, but not totally covered, in a red 'silk' robe with an Oriental pattern on it. This she wrapped around her thick, unwashed body as she eyed the pair.

"I don't do threesomes," she said firmly, her breath reeking of alcohol. "It'll be one at a time or none at all. And I get paid up front so's ya'll can't fleece me." She put out one hand and wiggled her fingers as if expecting the cash then and there.

Noah smirked and held up his badge. "Carmen Meeks?"

Her eyes flicked to the badge then back to Noah. "Oh, hell," she said, holding out her hands, wrists together.

"I'll take that as a yes," Noah said, putting his badge away and retrieving a pair of handcuffs. "Carmen Meeks, we're taking you down to the station for questioning in connection with the hit-and-run death of Tasha Bailey earlier today-"

"Wait a minnit!" Carmen jerked her hands away before Noah could cuff her. "I don't know nuthin' about no hit-and-runs."

Noah grabbed her arm and slapped one handcuff on her wrist. "Well, then, you're under arrest for solicitation. Of two police officers, nonetheless." Noah maneuvered her hands behind her back to cuff the other wrist, putting her face rather squarely in Franks'.

"You're a perty one, ain't ya? What's yer name, sweet pea?" Carmen asked, her breath hitting him full force.

"Detective Franks, ma'am," he replied uncomfortably.

"Ma'am? And good manners on him, too. Sugar," she called back over her shoulder to Noah, "you sure you wouldn't let me have a few minutes with yer friend here before the unpleasantness?"

Noah peered over her shoulder at Franks. "Oh, I don't know, Carmen – I just got him today and wouldn't want him worn out before his first day is done."

She turned back to Franks. "Shame and all, really. I'd be willing to not charge ya, just this once," she added with what she must have thought was a seductive wink. Franks' face apparently was as red as he feared it was, for she cackled. "Oh, lor' – look at 'im blush! Ain't you just precious – Frankie, was it?"

"Franks, ma'am," he corrected. To Noah he said, "I think we should get going, we wouldn't want Ms. Meeks to catch a chill."

Noah grinned unabashedly. "Heaven forbid," he said, steering Carmen toward the car and reading her rights.

CHAPTER SIX

———

CARMEN WAS STILL FAR from sober. She huddled in the uncomfortable metal chair pushed several feet back from the wooden table in Interview Room B. Her robe covered her, hanging down to her ankles, but, as she sat cross-legged, it left her right leg bare to the cool air of the room. She dangled her right foot, almost shaking the fuzzy slipper right off, and stared at the ground, mumbling to herself incomprehensively.

Franks turned away from the one-way window that overlooked the interview room. "You're sure you don't wanna do this?"

Noah shook his head. "She likes you. I think a little 'good cop' would get us pretty far with her – and no, that was not another innuendo at your expense," he added with a glint in his eyes that suggested otherwise. Noah flipped on the camera that would record the interview session.

Franks sighed, then squared his shoulders and exited the observation room. A moment later, he entered the room where Carmen sat. "Sorry to keep you waiting," he said using an accent that was somewhere between his typical speaking voice and his natural accent, being as calming and friendly as possible. He walked to the chair on the opposite side of the table and started to sit down. Instead, he made a point of letting Carmen catch him noticing her bare leg.

"It's a little chilly in here, don't ya think? I can turn the heat up just a bit if you'd like."

She eyed him warily. "Sure thing, sweet pea."

31

Franks went to the thermostat and unlocked its cover. He bumped up the temperature a few degrees, then locked the cover back into place. "That'll be better in a minute."

She nodded, but otherwise ignored him, choosing to stare at the floor instead. Franks sat across from her and looked at her a long moment without saying a word. She was aware of his gaze, and though she tried to act like it didn't matter, began to sit up a little straighter and composed her expression to its most attractive. "So, Carmen – may I call you Carmen or would you prefer Miss Meeks?"

She lifted her eyes to him. "I suppose Carmen is all right with me, Frankie."

"Now, Carmen, I'm willing to bet you meant what you said to my partner earlier about not knowing about the accident that killed that poor little girl today. At least, not knowing anything firsthand about it. But I do think you probably know a little more than you're letting on. Am I right?"

She started jiggling her foot again. "I told you already I don't."

He leaned across the table toward her and put on his best charming smile. "Oh, come on, Carmen. It's just us here; you can tell me the truth. You know who was driving your car today, don't you?"

"It wasn't me!"

"No?"

"No!" She gave him a very direct stare.

"Were you in the car with him, though, at the time?"

"No! And I was very upset to find out he'd even taken it again without me knowing ahead of time. I mean, some people can be just plain rude and thoughtless at times, ain't they?"

He latched onto her slip up. "Does he take your car without permission a lot?"

She opened her mouth, and then shut it abruptly. "Oh, you're a slick one, ain't ya, Frankie? I'm not sayin' nuthin' about him."

Franks smiled. "All right. Let's talk about something else then. When we found your car, there were beer bottles, some pills and lots of other naughty things left behind. Now, my partner thinks it all belongs to you. If that's true, then you're fixin' to do some serious jail time. But if it's not true, and it all belongs to someone else, then you'll need to tell us now before this goes any further."

Her foot jiggling was at a mad pace now. "I don't think I wanna talk to you anymore."

He sighed tragically. "Now don't be like that, Carmen. I'm tryin' to help you."

"If that were true, you wouldn't ask me about him. People like him can do whatever they want and nuthin' can touch them. People like me, well we can disappear and nobody'd care."

Franks furrowed his brow. He didn't know who she was talking about, but he understood that whoever it was, he was either really rich or really powerful – or both. Even though he had never worked in Vice, he knew enough about women like Carmen to realize what she said was true. It was hard to admit, but the disappearance of a prostitute didn't get as much attention devoted to it as the disappearance of, say, a housewife or high school girl. It was a harsh reality, and one not likely to change, no matter what he thought.

"Carmen, I can promise you that, if you help us, we can protect you." She scoffed and turned away from him. He slid his chair over to put himself in her line of sight again. "I mean it. Do the right thing here, Carmen. A little girl is dead because of this guy. There's no reason you should protect him."

"I ain't protectin' *him*, I'm protectin' *me*!" She wiped away a tear that slipped free of her lashes.

"Let us protect you. I promise -"

"You can shove your promises; I know how it would end." She glared at him, hard, and he knew he was losing her.

He sighed. "I need a drink. Can I get you anything?"

She narrowed her eyes, but then shook her hair back and asked, "You got any diet soda?"

"I'm sure we do. I'll be right back." He got up and left the interrogation room, rejoining Noah in the adjoining observation room.

Noah looked almost puzzled. "Why did you leave? She was starting to cave."

"Really? Because that's not what I saw. I see a scared woman who's going to keep her mouth shut tight to keep her head." He shook his head. "I'm getting nowhere, man."

"You have to keep pushing her. She'll break, I promise." He faced the glass again. "And if you don't break her, I will. But she won't like my approach nearly as much as yours."

"She's terrified! She's not going to give us anything as long as she thinks she's in danger – and she's convinced we can't, or won't, do anything to protect her. Why don't you and your buddy at the lab just work your magic, get us something concrete that leads us to the guy who's actually the criminal here? We don't need to put her in this position."

Noah turned on him, his eyes hard. "You better watch yourself, *Frankie*," he said, using Carmen's pet name for him. "You don't get to come in here and tell me how to run my investigation." He jabbed his finger toward the glass. "She knows who killed that little girl and she is going to tell us." His voice was on the verge of yelling. "You are going to do your damn job and make her! Are we clear?"

Anger and adrenaline surged through him, making him want to punch Noah in the face. Instead, he got right back in his face, shoving him until his back was against the glass, and said, "You back off. Now. You may have forced your old partner to deal with your crap, but I am not going to put up with it. Back. Off."

Noah looked like he'd been gut-punched. All the anger dissipated from his eyes, only to be replaced by grief. It may not have been the best way to go about it, but he knew he had to rein him in, at least a little, if the two of them were going to be able to stand each other.

Noah gritted his teeth. "I'm going in there. You lost your chance." He shoved past Franks and headed toward the door.

"Harkham, wait," Franks said. Noah stopped but didn't turn around. "Let me go with you. Let me play her ally. Bullying her alone isn't going to work."

Noah jerked the door open. "Don't forget her drink."

CHAPTER SEVEN

————

"DO YOU WANT TO GO TO jail, Carmen?" Noah leaned over her shoulder, his face a fraction of an inch from hers. He kept his voice calm and low, but only because he knew that was often more unsettling than yelling.

She shifted uncomfortably. "No. But I don't wanna die, neither."

"Tasha Bailey didn't want to die, either," he pressed, coming around to kneel in front of her. "A witness heard her scream, just once, before her short little life was taken from her. She died scared and alone, Carmen. She was only eleven years old."

Tears spilled from her eyes. She wiped them furiously. "You tryin' t'make me cry? Well, congralutations," she slurred. "You got it. But that don't change the fact that I had nuthin' to do with what happened to that little girl!"

Noah slammed his hand on the table next to her, making her jump like she'd stepped on a live wire. "But you KNOW who did!"

"NO!"

"TELL US WHO KILLED HER!"

"Harkham, give her some room," Franks said, laying a hand on Noah's arm. The unexpected physical contact broke Noah's concentration. He shot a furious look at his new partner, but shrugged him off and walked a few feet away anyway.

"We can help you, Carmen, but only if you help us," Noah said, weariness creeping into his voice. "We won't let anyone get to you and we'll never let you out of our sight until this is over. Okay? Just tell us who killed that little girl."

"And what happens after you put him away? Or if you find him but don't have enough evidence to put him away for good? Who do you think he's gonna come after?" She began to weep. She may have still been a touch drunk, her words slurring more often than not, but she was together enough to be scared witless.

Noah chafed at the thought of the time they were wasting, the opportunities they were losing out on. This guy was out there somewhere, knowing full well he killed someone and taking whatever steps he could to prevent his being caught for it. He turned around and grabbed her by her arm. "Stand up," he ordered.

"Harkham, what the –" Franks started.

"I told you coddling her was a waste of time. She's going down for prostitution."

"Hey! I ain't done nuthin!" Carmen protested.

"Honey, you said you'd do us one at a time if we paid you up front. That's called solicitation in my book." He jerked her to her feet. "Besides, whoever this guy is will probably figure out that we found your car and picked you up. Do you think he'd believe you when you said you didn't talk? Trust me; jail's going to be a lot safer for you."

Carmen trembled from head to toe. "But you can't...I mean, you have to say I didn't tell you anything! You can't pretend I did, he'll kill me! Even in jail, he can get to me."

"Who, Carmen? Who is this guy that he's that powerful?" Franks asked, coming over to her other side.

She looked from Noah to Franks, torn by what to do. Her pale lips quivered. She ran her tongue over her dry lips. "Okay," she eventually said. "Evan Dalton. His name is Evan Dalton." She sagged against Noah's grip.

Franks looked at Noah. "Do you know this guy?"

Noah thought a moment. He went cold when he made the connection. "Carmen, think carefully: do you mean Jonathan Dalton's son?"

She nodded. "See what I mean? You might as well kill me now and get it over with."

"Why? Who is Jonathan Dalton?" Franks asked.

Noah let go of Carmen's arm. "Jonathan Dalton owns about half the real estate in Riverdale. He's one of the richest, most powerful men in this city. In the last five years, he's been suspected of being behind the death or disappearance of at least three people who had gone up against him one way or another. Nothing has ever been proven, so he still gets to breathe free air..." He headed for the door. "We need to take this to the Captain."

"What about me?" Carmen called after him.

"Just sit tight, ma'am, we'll get this figured out," Franks assured her before leaving with Noah.

Once out in the hall, Noah let out a frustrated growl and slapped a palm against the wall. "This can't be happening," he groaned.

"So he's rich and corrupt, he's not above the law," Franks said. "We take him down just like any other crook and case closed."

Noah furrowed his brows. "Are you really that naïve? We can't touch this guy, not with a million eye-witnesses, all the evidence we could ever hope for and a signed confession, got it? He's not just rich, he's connected. He's powerful. And Carmen's right: we signed her death warrant the second we knocked on her door. This can NOT be happening."

He let out another growl of frustration. The last thing he could afford was another cold case. Ziehring never said it, but Noah knew his failure to find the killer he and Rob had been chasing had counted against him. *If I don't close this case...* He shook his head; he was not about to let that happen. He just had to find the right way.

CHAPTER EIGHT

―――

THE FOLLOWING AFTERNOON, Noah, Franks and Captain Ziehring were discussing the possibility of police or federal protection for Carmen and how best to approach the arrest of Evan Dalton.

"We'll have to do this as under the radar as possible," Ziehring said with a weary sigh. "I say we go in with the pretense that we have intel that says Evan may have been in the area and we're hoping he might have seen something that could help us. We ask him to come down here to make a statement. Once he's here, we present him with Carmen's story –"

"Keeping her name and anything that could lead him back to her out of it, though, right?" Franks asked.

"Of course. There's no reason for him to know we got our information from her until it goes to trial."

"If it ever does," Noah grumbled. "This is all great, but until the lab turns up prints or DNA that we know belongs to him we don't have anything to hold him on except the testimony of a drunken prostitute. That is never gonna fly, Captain, and you know it." He chafed his palms on the arms of his chair. He felt nervous, like Dalton was already slipping through his fingers. He itched to get out and do something, even though he knew there was nothing he could do at that point.

"Then I suggest you get over to the lab and see if Parker needs a hand."

Noah looked at Franks. "Maybe you can get your girlfriend to sit with a sketch artist. I'd love to be able to shove that rich punk's picture in his face and ask him to explain how a prostitute knows his face in so much detail." He got to his feet and headed toward the door.

"I'll talk to her," Franks replied.

Ziehring picked up his phone. "I'll see if I can get someone down here by the end of the day," he said as Noah left the room.

WHEN NOAH ARRIVED AT the lab's garage, he found Cal Parker - the crime lab day shift supervisor – in the midst of cataloging every object that had been found inside the car. He wore a full-body Tyvek suit and mask that left only his hazel eyes visible as he looked up from rooting around in the back passenger side floorboard. "Ah, Noah," he said, "I think you read my mind: I could use another set of hands in here."

"That's what I'm here for," Noah replied, heading to the cabinet where other suits like the one Parker wore were stored. He slipped one on and donned a pair of gloves as well before joining the criminalist at the car. "Tell me we've got good stuff in here, Parker," he said.

Parker straightened his somewhat tall frame and gestured toward the long table where he already had multiple evidence bags laid out. "Someone had quite the party in here. We've got bottles of beer, champagne and wine. We've got ecstasy, valium and speed. There's also a slew of little bags of a mysterious white powder still in the car," he continued, "and a couple of joints for good measure."

"Great, so we should get a decent amount of fingerprints. What about DNA?"

Parker grabbed a handheld UV light and switched it on inside the car. As he shone the light across the back seat, several small stains – remnants of Carmen's recent job-related activities – fluoresced brightly. "That's why I need another pair of hands - we've got all of those to collect samples of, too."

"Great," Noah said.

"Like I said, someone had quite the party."

Photographing, collecting and labeling all the rest of the evidence in Carmen's car took the better part of the rest of the day. When they were finished, Noah helped Parker log everything in. The lab techs would handle the actual processing of the prints and DNA, but Parker and Conrad Ward would do the comparison of the paint and brake fluid from the car to that found at the scene. Once there was a suspect in custody, they would also make the comparison between his prints and DNA to that found in the car.

Satisfied that everything was well in hand for the time being, Noah decided to grab a late dinner and then get back to the station and see how the sketch was coming along. He wanted Evan Dalton in custody as quickly as possible and was frustrated that he had to handle it with kid gloves instead of busting in and slapping the cuffs on him. When he got back, he found Carmen sitting in the conference room with the sketch artist. Ziehring and Franks stood just outside, watching the proceedings through the window.

"How is she doing in there?" Noah asked his captain.

Both men turned around at the sound of his voice. "So far, so good," Ziehring replied. "Looks like they're finishing up."

"Did she give you any trouble about going through with this?"

"Not really," Franks answered. "She's scared, of course, but I also think she realizes how important this is. Plus, I get the feeling she doesn't like this Dalton kid and is getting a little satisfaction from the prospect of helping to put him away." He shrugged. "Either that or she's recognized the fact that, as long as she's cooperative, she gets a bed and somewhat decent food."

Noah nodded. "Good. Where are we with the arrest warrant?"

"It's in play," Ziehring said. "But remember: you're only asking him down here to help with the investigation, as far as he's concerned, until we know for sure he's behind this. Just because he borrowed Carmen's car may not necessarily mean he was the one driving when the victim was hit."

The sketch artist looked up and nodded to the trio standing outside the conference room. Both Noah and Franks went in.

"Here you are, Detectives," the artist, Joe McDonnell, said, handing over the sketch Carmen had helped him create. Noah studied it. He had never seen Evan Dalton except on rare occasions when some paparazzi were able to snap a photo of the millionaire, and even then he usually had part of his face covered. But the face in the sketch did bear a strong resemblance.

Noah felt the first real piece needed to close this case fall into place. He looked at Franks. "Let's go."

"Whoa, Harkham - it's after eleven," Franks protested.

"So?" Noah asked. "He's filthy rich and can do whatever he wants - do you honestly think he's at home in bed?" Carmen scoffed at that.

Franks opened the door and gestured for Noah to step outside with him. He shut the door behind them and lowered his voice. "Look, I'm just saying if we're going to make our cover story work, we can't barge in and drag him away from whatever he may be doing this time of night. Let's just go home and pick him up in the morning."

Noah let out a deep breath. He knew Franks was right, but the thought of waiting any longer frustrated him to no end. "All right, fine," he conceded.

Franks held out his hand. "I've pulled Dalton's BMV record. I'll compare her sketch to his license photo; just to be sure before we go off half-cocked."

Noah handed him the sketch. "Knock yourself out." He turned and walked down the hall.

"Where are you going?" Franks called after him.

"Home."

CHAPTER NINE

———

IT WASN'T UNTIL HE pulled up outside the huge, almost mansion-like, gated house that Noah remembered that he had picked Franks up. He had, in effect, left his new partner stranded back at the station, unless he either got a ride with one of the uniformed officers or called a taxi. He did feel a little guilty about that, since it was likely to make Franks the object of some of the other cops' ridicule for a short while, but Noah knew it was better for Franks to be mad at him about that little faux pas than for him to know what he was really doing right now...

He turned off the ignition and settled in. The unmarked car he'd taken from the department's motor pool had seen a lot of use and was comfortably broken in. He reached for his travel mug, filled with strong black tea, and took a long drink. The night was still cool, but the rain had at last stopped, leaving a somber lacquer on everything it had touched. The house he watched was dark and quiet, giving the impression that it was empty. But even if that were true, Noah knew Evan Dalton had to come home sometime.

This wasn't his first stakeout, and, as the stillness settled over him, he thought about previous stakeouts he'd been on with his first partner. Rob had a no-nonsense kind of attitude, but a heart as big as the sky, and he treated people with unfailing kindness with no expectation of being treated in kind. He always somehow managed to make the criminals he put away feel not only guilty for what they had done, but also reassured there was a chance it was all going to be okay someday. Noah had never been able to master that talent, but that was part of what made the two such an effective pair. Noah could play the hardnosed figure of retribution, while Rob was the symbol of redemption.

It irritated him to find he could see a lot of Rob's spirit in Franks. He didn't want to like this guy, and it hurt like hell having him remind him so much of Rob without being the real thing. He sighed. There were more important things to worry about right now.

He opened his glove compartment and retrieved a set of binoculars. He trained them on the upper windows of the house, then those on the lower floor, but saw no signs of anyone inside. It was a little after 12:30, but he was sure the Dalton's would not be asleep already. He lowered the binoculars and frowned. What if they had left town to avoid the cops? What if they were already in another state – or another country? If no one showed by morning, he'd check with the airports.

Two hours later, his eyelids were begging him to let them close. He stretched and yawned, then shook his head to dispel the drowsiness. Headlights coming his way caught his attention. A sleek sedan with tinted windows pulled into the drive at the Dalton's house, pausing a moment while the huge wrought iron gate swung open, then continued up to the porte-cochere. Three well-dressed figures exited the vehicle from passenger seats, and the driver drove on around to the garage at the side of the house.

Noah peered through the binoculars at the two men and one woman headed for the front door. One of the men appeared to be in his fifties, with a stocky build and blonde hair touched with grey. This Noah knew was Jonathan Dalton; his photograph was always in the news, for one new building project or another. The other man looked much younger, in his early twenties Noah estimated, with darker hair and movie star good looks. He matched the sketch Carmen had given them almost exactly: Evan Dalton.

He wanted to get out right then and confront this child killer before he could retreat to the comfort of his bed, but, at the last moment, sense won out over instinct. Instead, he settled back in his seat and watched...

HIS CELL PHONE JARRED him awake. With a sharp curse at himself for falling asleep, he grabbed up his phone. "Harkham," he answered sleepily.

"Harkham, where are you?"

It was Ziehring. "I was asleep. What's going on?"

"You wouldn't happen to be taking your nap outside the Dalton's house, would you?"

He closed his eyes and sighed. Crap. He glanced at the clock: 7:12. "I came by to talk to him, like we said, but they weren't home. Guess I fell asleep waiting for them."

This time Ziehring sighed. "Noah..." he sounded drained. "You came this close to being picked up by uniformed officers. Jonathan Dalton called the police a few minutes ago because he said some guy had been watching his house all night."

"I'll go talk to them, apologize and explain everything," Noah offered. "I can fix it, sir."

"Franks is on his way. Sit tight until he gets there, then you both can go talk to the Daltons."

Noah's hand clenched tighter around the phone. "Sir, I don't need Franks to chaperone me. This is my investigation."

"After last night, I'd say you're pretty lucky that that's still true. I said kid gloves on this one. If you want me to believe I can trust you alone, you've gotta get your act together. Until then, your partner is gonna be there every step of the way."

His tone brooked no argument, so Noah didn't make any. "Yes, sir," he replied through gritted teeth.

"That's all I wanted to hear," Ziehring said before disconnecting.

Noah pocketed his phone and slammed his hand against the steering wheel. His anger still smoldered ten minutes later when Franks arrived. Noah got out of the car and was halfway across the street before Franks exited his car. "Harkham," he called, hurrying to catch up.

"Let's just do this," Noah answered.

They got to the gate and Noah pressed the button on the intercom mounted at the edge of the drive. "What do you want?" a gruff, military-like voice demanded.

A camera was built in to the security unit and Noah held his badge before its lens. "RPD, open the gate, please, sir."

"What's this about?"

"We need to speak with Evan Dalton. We're hoping he can help us with one of our investigations," Noah answered, putting his badge away.

"Is that why you surveilled the house all night, Detective...?"

"Detective Sergeant Noah Harkham, sir. And I can explain last night, if you'd kindly let us in. It's a bit too chilly this morning to stand out here and discuss it."

There was a long pause, and then the gate rattled open. "Thank you," Noah said before he and Franks proceeded up to the house. It was even grander up close; the word stately kept coming to mind.

"Nicely done," Franks commented.

Noah just grunted, still a bit sleepy. "Do you have the sketch?"

Franks patted the pocket of his long, lightweight black pea coat. "Right here."

"Good. We won't need it just yet, but keep it close by." He took the three wide, shallow stone steps at a trot and raised a hand to knock. Before he could, however, the door swung open and he was face to face with a dour-faced man built like a bullet in a stripped-down tactical suit.

"Detectives, I'm Waylon Smith, head of security. This way, please," Smith stepped aside and eyed them warily as they passed. It had been him on the intercom, and Noah could see he ran a very secure operation, which led Noah to speculate about why Jonathan Dalton had bothered calling the police instead of siccing Smith on him. He guided them through the tile floored grand foyer, past a mahogany staircase so polished it gave off a warm glow and to a formal sitting room decorated in style to rival the Biltmore Mansion. A cream-colored couch with tone-on-tone floral design sat to one side, and it was to this Smith led them.

Noah and Franks sat down; Smith settled into a stance that Noah guessed was supposed to be intimidating a few feet away. "Now," Smith said, "what exactly is it you want with young Mr. Dalton?"

"We have reason to believe he may have been in the vicinity of an accident that occurred yesterday," Franks answered, meeting Smith's direct gaze unflinchingly. "We're hoping he may be able to help us with our investigation."

"And you are?"

"Detective Alan Franks."

"Tell me, Detectives," Smith continued, "is it normal RPD protocol to put the house of someone who may have been a witness to a crime under surveillance?"

Noah shifted in his seat. "I apologize for that, but it wasn't like that. I came by to ask for Evan's assistance last night, but no one was home. I decided to wait until he returned, but I, uh, I fell asleep," he added with a self-deprecating laugh. "It was a long day yesterday."

"Uh-huh."

"I assure you, Mr. Smith; I had no intention of sleeping in that car when I got here last night." Noah held Smith's gaze with as reassuring and placid an expression as he could muster.

Smith stared at him a long moment. "Wait here, I'll see if Evan is awake."

He exited the room, leaving the two detectives on their own. An uncomfortable silence fell between them. "So is that really what happened?" Franks asked.

"What are you talking about?"

"Last night, Harkham. Surveilling the place," Franks answered.

Noah sat back and rubbed his hands across his face. "You heard what I said," he snapped.

"Yeah, I did, but my question still stands." He kept his gaze fixed on Noah, one eyebrow slightly lifted.

"Leave it, Franks."

"I would've backed you up, you know, if you'd insisted this was the right play. You didn't give me the chance."

"Please," Noah scoffed. "You would've backed my play? You haven't agreed with how I've done anything on this investigation so far – why would this be any different? I bet you were all over it when Ziehring gave you babysitting duty."

"That's not –"

"Good morning, Detectives," came a voice from just outside the room. The same young man Noah had seen entering the house last night stepped across the threshold. He was dressed in expensive wine-colored pajamas with a matching real silk robe cinched around his narrow waist. He sat himself wearily on the upholstered ottoman in front of the couch. "What can I do for you so early?"

"I apologize for waking you, but we were hoping you could help us out with something," Noah said.

"Uh, yeah, sure - what do you need? I mean, I already made a sizable contribution to the police department just last month, but if there's something you guys need–"

Noah held up a hand. "No, no - it's nothing like that, although I would like to offer my gratitude on behalf of the precinct for your support." It galled to play nice like this, but he knew he had to play it cool or he'd lose any chance they had to solve this case.

"Then I don't get what I can do for you." He yawned languidly.

"We were led to believe that you may have been in the vicinity of a tragic accident in James Park yesterday a little before four p.m.," Franks said. "We were hoping you could tell us if you saw or heard anything that might help us out."

His face scrunched in confusion. "James Park? Why would I be out there? I mean, what is there even to do in James Park, anyway? Isn't it just a bunch of middle-class houses?" He noticed some lint on his shirt and plucked it off.

"It's a neighborhood, yes," Franks said, somewhat defensively, Noah thought.

"So you're saying you weren't there?" Noah asked.

"No," Evan replied as if the very idea was ridiculous. "I attended a couple of different charity events yesterday. They kept me busy until quite late last night, as you know," he added, casting a look at Noah.

Noah nodded toward Franks' pocket and held his hand out until Franks retrieved the sketch and handed it over. He unfolded the paper and held it up for Evan to see. "This isn't you, then?"

Evan leaned forward and studied the drawing a moment, then leaned back and looked at the two detectives as if they'd lost their minds. "I hope you're not serious," he said with an incredulous smile. "That? That is not me, and, frankly, I'm a little offended anyone would even think so." Despite this denial, Noah thought for just a moment that there had been a flicker of... something behind Evan's eyes.

Noah frowned and looked at the sketch again. It was remarkably similar to Evan, but he did see some significant differences that he had at first chalked up to Carmen's drug- and alcohol-impaired memory. The face in the sketch was not as refined as Evan's, and the shape of the nose was quite different. "Well, then we're very sorry to have disturbed you," Noah said, putting the sketch away. He affected his most apologetic expression. "However, I'm afraid we'll still need you to come down to the station with us anyway, just to clear this all up."

"What are you talking about? I wasn't there, so there's nothing to clear up." He sat straighter and crossed his arms.

"It's just a formality," Franks said.

"Right," Noah agreed, spreading his hands. "We just need to get a formal statement from you saying where you were yesterday afternoon, so we can strike you from our witness list."

Evan nodded slowly as if trying to decide whether to cooperate. "Okay, I guess. I mean, I don't see the point of all this, but whatever you need. God forbid I stand in the way of bureaucracy," he added with a wink. He stood up - the detectives following suit – and gestured toward the door. "I'll just go get dressed."

"We really appreciate this, Mr. Dalton," Noah said.

"Ah, please, I just wish I had been there and could help you guys out." He started out of the room, but turned back. "By the way, what is it that happened? What was I supposed to have been a witness to?"

"A hit-and-run," Noah answered, watching his reaction closely. "An eleven year old girl was struck by a car and killed."

Evan's face paled. "That's...that's awful. I...I wish I had been there. Maybe I could have stopped it." He gave a sad smile before leaving the room.

"Is it just me or does he know a lot more than he's telling us?" Frank asked, once they were alone.

"Definitely."

A few minutes later, Noah, Franks and Evan were at the end of the drive, waiting as the gate opened. Behind them, over the sound of the gate's mechanisms, came a booming voice that demanded, "Where the hell do you think you're taking my son?"

They turned to see a stocky man that looked like a college jock gone to seed. "Dad, what are you doing?" Evan asked.

Jonathan Dalton pushed past his son and got right up in Franks' face. "If you think you can just waltz into my home and harass my family, you better think again," he shouted. "I'll have your badge for this!"

"Sir, your son agreed to come with us," Franks explained. "He is not under arrest."

Dalton turned on his son then. "What did I tell you? Never, never talk to cops without a lawyer! Are you that dense, Evan? Come on, we're going back inside." He grabbed Evan's arm so hard the young man had to stifle a cry.

Noah stepped forward, putting one hand on Dalton's forearm and the other on the gun holstered at his hip. "Sir, take your hand off him and walk away."

Dalton looked at Noah's hand on his arm, then fixed his gaze on the gun Noah was about to draw. "This is insane!" Dalton said, his teeth gritted and his face turning a livid red. "What are your names?"

"Detective Sergeant Noah Harkham. I am the ranking officer here - if you have anything to say about what's happening here, you file against me. But, as your son is an adult and has agreed to come with us willingly to sort this all out, you cannot stop him from doing so. And if you hurt him one more time, you'll be under arrest for assault. Are we clear on that, Mr. Dalton?"

Dalton jerked his hand away and pulled a cell phone out of his pocket, walked a few paces away, and dialed. "It's Dalton. Evan's gotten himself mixed up in something and two detectives are here hauling him out of the house. Get down to precinct number..." he looked at Noah, who held up five fingers, though he kept his thumb held ambiguously close to the side of his hand, "four and sort this out. Now." He didn't leave any time for a reply before hanging up.

He turned back to Noah and jabbed a finger at him. Noah just gazed back impassively and whatever retort Dalton was about to say withered on his lips. He glared at Evan before walking away.

Evan gave a weak laugh. "Don't pay my dad any attention. He's just really protective."

Franks smiled. "He must love you very much," he said, the sarcasm undisguised.

Noah gestured for them to exit the gate, putting Evan between Franks and himself. Evan chatted as they walked, but he seemed to be suppressing nervous energy. "He's not always like that, you know. He must think I'm in some kind of trouble, which will only embarrass the family. And that can't be abided," he added, mimicking his father flawlessly.

Noah nodded. This lined up with everything he'd heard about Jonathan Dalton. They were going to have to be more careful from here on out. Well, he was going to have to be more careful; Franks had done just fine. But it just meant they needed to do everything to keep Carmen's identity secret, even if it turns out Evan wasn't involved...or maybe even especially if he wasn't.

Franks looked at Noah and said very quietly, "The fourth precinct?"

Noah grinned. "Hey, I held up five fingers. It's not my fault he didn't see them all."

CHAPTER TEN

———

"ARE YOU SURE HE WON'T be able t'see me?" Carmen asked. She was now sober, washed and dressed in a sweatshirt and sweat pants that bore the Riverdale PD logo. She, Noah and Franks stood in the observation room that overlooked the same interview room she had occupied just the other night.

"I promise," Franks answered.

She still looked unsure, but finally nodded. "Okay."

Franks nodded to Noah, who raised the blinds covering the window. Evan Dalton sat at the table, writing out his statement. Carmen took a deep breath and looked at him closely.

Franks watched her closely as well. Her brow furrowed and she let out the pent-up breath. "Wait - Frankie, who's that?"

Franks frowned in confusion. "That's Evan Dalton."

She looked at him like he'd grown a second head. "I don't mean t'tell ya yer job, sweet pea, but I think you need to check yer records. I don't know who that young man is. I wouldn't mind getting t'know him, though – he is quite the tasty little –"

"Carmen," Noah interrupted, "are you sure about this?"

"Positive. He looks a lot like Evan, but, like, ten times better lookin'."

"That's Evan Dalton, so who the hell are we looking for?" Noah asked.

Franks looked at him. "I compared the sketch to his DMV photo, and I still thought it was this guy."

Noah nodded. "I know; me, too."

"I should probably cancel the warrant for his phone records."

"Actually, maybe we should hold off on that," Noah mused. "We both saw Evan's reaction to that sketch. He knows that guy and he's bound to contact him."

Franks looked at Carmen. "We'll be right back, Carmen." He tilted his head toward the door.

Noah followed Franks out into the hall. "What you're talking about isn't exactly legal," Franks said. "We need something more than his reaction to give us probable cause."

"Technically, yes. But if we push Evan into revealing his connection to this guy, we can look at him as an accessory after the fact and then there's our probable cause."

Franks sucked in a breath and mulled this over. "That's really slippery, Harkham."

Noah leaned toward him, reaching his hands out almost beseechingly. "But if he goes for it, then it gives us all we need."

Franks debated a moment. If he wanted to cement his position as Noah's partner, now was the time to show Noah he trusted him. It was tricky, what he had planned, but he felt he knew enough about the man to see that he would never do anything blatantly illegal. Bending the law, using what loopholes already existed – all for the greater good of putting a very bad criminal away – yes, but Noah respected the law too much to break it. "What do you want me to do?"

Noah visibly relaxed. "Reasonable deception. I just need you to follow my lead." He started to open the door, but stopped. Without looking back he said, "I want you to know I appreciate this."

"No problem," Franks replied.

Noah nodded and opened the door to the room where Carmen waited. "Carmen, you can go back to the lounge now." He held the door open for her and pointed to the nearest uniformed officer he could see. "Just tell that officer there I said to take you back and get you whatever you need. It won't be much longer now and we'll get you to a safe house, I promise."

She looked at him, skeptical, but exited the room all the same. "What about the other Evan Dalton? My Evan Dalton? I mean, how are you going to find him, if that darlin' in there is the real one? And who in their right mind would even try to steal his identity? They must have a death wish," she added with a shudder.

"That's what we're hoping to find out," Franks reassured her. He motioned the officer over to escort her back.

When Carmen was gone, the two entered the interview room. Evan put down the can of Coke he'd been drinking from and smiled at them. He gestured to the form he'd been filling out.

"I'm all through with this."

"That's great, but I'm afraid we've hit a small snag," Noah said apologetically as he and Franks sat across from Evan.

"Oh? What kind of snag?"

"Well, we've had a positive identification. The witness we told you about is here and we know that you were in James Park yesterday. In fact, we know that it was you driving the car that killed that little girl, and right now we're processing fingerprints that will prove it."

Evan stared, incredulous. Then he let out a disbelieving laugh. "That's insane! I wasn't anywhere near that place yesterday or any other day. Is this a joke?"

Franks leaned forward, resting his arms on the table. "No joke, Evan. The witness was very specific: Evan Dalton was driving that car."

The young man went pale and began to sweat. "No, no that can't be – they must have made a mistake – or maybe they're just looking for money. Yeah, they must be trying to blackmail me or something." He looked back and forth between the two detectives, and they just looked back impassively. "I swear! I'm being framed here, can't you see that?"

"Then give me some other explanation, Evan," Noah replied. "Tell me how this witness could make a sketch that so closely resembles your face and give us your name if you had nothing to do with this?" Noah withdrew the sketch from his inner jacket pocket and slid it over to Evan.

Evan looked down at the sketch and fidgeted. "Look, that is not me. I did NOT do this!" He looked around frantically. "Where is my lawyer?"

"I'm sure he just got held up in traffic," Franks said laconically.

"Evan, if what you say is true, you gotta give us something to prove it. I mean, if you know who this other guy is – this guy you say is framing you – then we'll check it out. If what you say is true, we'll pick him up and you'll be cleared. It's that easy." He leaned back in his chair and crossed his arms. "But if you know who killed that little girl and you don't tell us, then that makes you an accessory after the fact. We can prosecute you for murder just the same as if you had actually been the one driving. Plus there's obstruction of justice –"

"Withholding evidence," Franks added.

"Not to mention wasting police time and anything else I can think of. And what will Daddy think then?"

Evan was near tears. "Look, man, I won't go to jail."

"Then tell us who this guy is," Franks prompted.

"No, you don't understand," Evan said. "I won't go to jail. That will not be allowed. And neither will he," he said, gesturing to the sketch.

"Your Daddy's money won't be enough to get you off for this," Noah said.

"Wait," Franks said, a realization coming over him in a sickening, cold wave. "Evan, are you trying to say that your father will do something to make sure you don't go to trial? Are you saying he'll hurt you?"

The tears slipped free and splattered the statement he had written. He wiped them away angrily and said nothing, looking at them a long, anguished moment. Then he nodded, once. "I'll disappear," he whispered. "Just like everyone else."

Franks sat back, floored. He and Noah exchanged a look. "We can protect you," Noah said.

Evan laughed, an almost hysterical sound. "No, you really can't."

"Evan, please," Franks pushed, "please tell us who did this. We can make sure that none of this comes back on you."

"How? The only way you would ever find him is through me and everyone will know it." He shook his head vehemently. "No, the only way neither of us gets hurt is if I keep my mouth shut. You can't prove I know this guy, so you can't charge me with anything. And if you try to charge me with murder, this sketch won't stand up in court once my lawyer gets done. That and my alibi will get me acquitted in record time." He shoved the Coke can toward Noah. "And the prints you'll get off of this won't match anything you got from the car, so that was a total waste of your time."

CHAPTER ELEVEN

———

FRANKS AND NOAH EXITED the interview room. The second the door was shut, Franks groaned and sagged against the wall. He looked over at Noah, who was standing a few feet away as if all the wind had been knocked out of his sails. "Now what?"

Noah flipped one hand toward the door. "He's right: we can't touch him. And if he won't give us the fake Evan Dalton, we're screwed."

"Not necessarily," Franks replied. "We have the warrant for his phone records. If they've been in contact, we can still get him." He rubbed his tired eyes with one hand. "Or maybe the actual killer will already be in the system and we'll get a hit off his prints. Any word on that from the lab?"

Noah shook his head. "Not yet." He took a deep breath and let it out audibly. "But you're right: our one shot is the physical evidence... On the off chance Evan changes his mind about helping us, though, I'm going to put in a call to the U.S. Marshals about protection until the trial. We'll need bigger guns than ours to keep this kid alive."

The sound of agitated voices interrupted them. A harried little man in a sharp suit rushed toward them, followed by an irritated uniformed officer. "Sir, you can't just –"

The man in the suit waved the officer off. "Like hell I can't! I demand to see my client." He quickened his pace when he saw Noah and Franks. "You," he said to Franks, "where is Evan Dalton?"

"And you are...?"

"Jeffrey Powell, I'm the Daltons' attorney. I demand to know who told Mr. Dalton that his son was being taken to the Fourth Precinct instead of the Fifth. I have spent the last thirty-five minutes talking in circles with a bunch of clueless uniformed idiots only to find out my client, Mr. Evan Dalton, is actually here. I demand answers!"

Noah stepped forward. "I apologize if there was any misunderstanding, Mr. Powell, but I assure you I gave Mr. Dalton the correct information. But you're here now, so everything is fine."

Powell raised one eyebrow and put one finger up to Noah's face. "Did you interrogate my client?"

"We talked a little," Noah said dismissively. Franks kept his expression neutral, just as Powell switched his gaze over from Noah.

"Oh," Powell replied with an ironic chuckle. "Oh, you'll be lucky to still have your badge when I'm through with you." He shot a dark look at Franks. "Both of you."

Franks decided to take a gamble. "Mr. Powell, do you represent Evan or Jonathan Dalton?" he asked, keeping his voice calm and pleasant.

"I represent any member of the Dalton family that needs my help, but mostly I work for Jonathan Dalton, yes." He relaxed his stance some, seeming intrigued by the question.

"What would happen if one member of the Dalton family needed representation in a situation where he or she might also need protection from another member of the family?"

Powell thought a moment, crinkling his brows over his dark brown eyes. "I'm not sure I understand the question."

Noah shot him a look of warning, but Franks put a hand out, gesturing for him to trust him on this. "Let me level with you: Evan is looking at some serious charges here. More than we thought when we picked him up earlier. But all of it could be avoided if he would agree to cooperate with us."

"I supposed you want him to just roll over and confess to whatever charges it is you're leveling against him, then?"

"Honestly, we just want him to stop protecting whoever it is he's protecting. All of the charges we're bringing against him stem from the fact that he refuses to tell us who killed a little girl yesterday – someone he knows is guilty. He's withholding evidence and impeding our investigation." Franks laid one hand on attorney's shoulder and turned him toward the door of the interview room. "We've offered protection, but he's too afraid to trust we can keep him safe. As his attorney, he needs you to have his best interest in mind."

"Dear God, what is he doing?" Powell started for the door, but hesitated. "Protect him from whom?" He looked at each detective in turn, then closed his eyes and waved one hand. "Never mind, I see exactly what you mean. And the answer, Detective, is I will always represent the one most in need. As long as I don't have to oppose any other member of the family in the courtroom, I see no conflict of interest here. Now, if you'll excuse me, I need to confer with my client."

He disappeared into the room with Evan. Noah looked at Franks and lifted his brows. "Come on, we need to check in with the lab and call the Marshals."

CHAPTER TWELVE

———

AFTER ABOUT TWENTY minutes, Powell exited the interview room and informed a uniformed officer that his client wanted to speak to Noah and Franks. The two entered the room, unsure what to expect.

"Have you contacted the U.S. Marshals?" Powell asked as soon as they entered.

"I have," Noah answered. "They are just waiting for your client's say so to proceed, but they are ready to offer him 24/7 protection from now until they feel the danger has passed."

Franks' stomach knotted just a little as he watched Evan struggle with his decision. He eventually nodded. Franks and Noah both let out a slow breath. "Okay," Franks said, "well, then the first thing –"

Powell held up a hand. "Get the Marshals here, get a protection plan detailed and hard evidence to compare to a suspect and then – and only then – will my client give you anything."

He looked at Evan protectively. "I'm afraid to say that Evan's fears are very much warranted. I can't say any more than that without breaking confidence, but rest assured I will do everything in my power to make sure he stays safe."

———

TWO HOURS LATER, TWO U.S. Marshals were closeted with Carmen and Evan, separately, under Captain Ziehring's supervision. Franks and Noah now had permission to pull Evan's phone records – thanks to Noah's persuasiveness – and were poring over the calls to and from Evan over the last week. Noah was on the phone to the lab every half hour or so, checking for updates on the prints and other evidence and Franks was starting to feel sorry for Conrad Ward and Cal Parker.

Noah had just gotten off the phone after his latest call to Conrad and finally looked pleased. "Minor victory, and one we already knew, but at least the evidence bears it out: Carmen's car was definitely the one that killed Tasha Bailey. Conrad matched the paint from her buttons to that on the car conclusively and verified the brake line was damaged. And there were hundreds of usable prints on objects inside the car. So far, no hits in AFIS for anyone matching any of the prints – other than Carmen, of course – but Conrad and Parker are still hard at work."

Franks was cross-referencing one particular call that had come in to Evan's phone around the time of the accident. He glanced up. "That's good."

"Did you find something?"

"Maybe," Franks said. "I'm running the number, but there was a fifteen second call made to Evan's phone at 3:43 yesterday." He looked back at the computer screen. "Here we go: the number is registered to Daniel Reed, cell phone." He noticed the address listed. "Take a guess where he lives."

Noah's expression turned even more satisfied. "James Park?"

Franks tapped the side of his nose. "Do you want to tell Evan and Powell?"

Noah shook his head. "Your break, your reveal."

Franks couldn't help but smile. "Be right back." He walked back to the room where Evan, Powell and one of the two Marshals were discussing the details of federal protection. The Marshal, a tall woman with long, straight brown hair and a very direct gaze, let Franks in. He looked at Evan, holding the phone records up. "Daniel Reed."

Evan's face told him the whole story before the young man could even speak. He struggled against some strong emotion. "Yeah," he answered, his voice breaking. "He's my half-brother."

Franks frowned. "Was your father married before? Did Daniel take his mother's name afterward?"

Evan gave Franks a look like you give to a very young or sweetly naïve person. "He's... what's that expression my grandmother would use? Ah, yes. Daniel was 'born on the wrong side of the blanket,' that's it."

"Ah, I see. Are you two close?"

"Not really. We never talked until this past year or two. Daniel has issues, Detective. He's not a bad guy, but he's got a drug habit, he drinks too much and he uses prostitutes. And those are just the problems I know about." Evan's face darkened. "Please be careful when you pick him up. If I have good reason to be afraid right now, Daniel should be terrified. He may be... uncooperative."

AFTER A QUICK LUNCH, Franks and Noah once again drove to the neighborhood of James Park. It was a sleepy little suburb much like the one he had grown up in, only a little more upscale. Franks' family had never been poor, but they had never been exactly well off either, but people like Evan Dalton still made him uncomfortable. That entitled attitude set his teeth on edge, as did the assumption that anyone who wasn't rolling in money was somehow less worthwhile.

But Evan seemed to come by it naturally. It wasn't as if he was a bad person – look at what he was willing to do to protect someone much less fortunate than himself. Granted, that person was a blood relative and Evan was actually protecting himself as much as, if not more than, Daniel Reed. Evan just seemed to take all the luxury and privilege he had enjoyed his whole life as a given, that there simply was no other way for him to live.

Noah disconnected the call he was on. "Backup is en route, just in case Mr. Reed decides to get squirrely on us."

"Good," Franks replied. His stomach knotted and jolts of buzzed energy coursed through his body. He drummed his fingers on the steering wheel as he passed a slow-moving semi.

"Are you okay?" Noah asked.

"Yeah, I'm good, it's just..." he trailed off as he eased the car back over into his lane.

"This is new territory," Noah finished for him. "Bringing in a killer."

Franks nodded. He dared a glance at Noah, expecting to see judgment behind his eyes, and was surprised to see understanding instead. "I've arrested over a hundred criminals just in my time in Atlanta," he explained, "but those were people who forged checks, stole identities and skimmed a bit off the top of the company's account. Not victimless crimes, but nothing like this, you know?" Noah nodded, so he continued. "I mean, what kind of person runs a child over and then just takes off? How can anyone be that heartless?"

Noah shook his head, his expression contemplative. "I don't have an answer for that. Everyone, me included, always assumes anyone who takes another person's life must be a soulless, evil person. But sometimes what happens is a product of circumstances beyond either party's control. It was 'kill or be killed' or they literally felt like there was no other option but to do what they did or to handle it the way they handled it afterward. These are people in extremis, desperate and scared. They aren't always cold-blooded. Although, I've seen my share of that type, too."

"And Daniel Reed? Do you think he's the first type or the second?"

"We can't know until we get the story from him, and even then..." he made a dismissive gesture. "It's different for every case. We just have to play it as it comes."

Franks glanced over at the address he had written in his notepad, which lay on the console between him and Noah. "I think this is it," he said, pulling up near a two-story Tudor style home. He shut off the car and turned toward Noah. "Do you want to wait for backup or just go on up?"

"They're right behind us, let's go. We may not need them at all."

"Okay," he agreed. They got out of the car and Franks popped the trunk where they had a pair of bulletproof vests and hands-free earpieces for their radios. They removed their suit jackets then strapped on the vests and inserted the earpieces – nicknamed 'earwigs' – into their ears. A quick systems check confirmed their radios were connected and ready to go. Franks checked the ammo in his sidearm before holstering it once more. Noah did the same and then looked him square in the eyes.

"Ready?" Noah asked.

"Ready."

"Okay. Dispatch, 2259 and 2914 are at the suspect's home. Approaching now," Noah reported, his voice coming to Franks both in person and through the earpiece. It was a little disorienting, but Franks ignored the effect.

"Copy that, 2259. Backup en route, ETA four minutes. Dispatch standing by."

"Okay, let's go," Noah said and then they were off, approaching Daniel Reed's house quickly and cautiously.

Franks kept his hand near his gun, but kept it holstered. He noticed Noah was doing the same, though he walked more confidently, scanning the area and taking everything in. Franks imitated his partner's demeanor, forcing himself to be more aware of his surroundings: the cars that lined the picturesque street, the cat that watched them from a fenced-in yard two houses down, the elderly man checking his mail across the street who now eyed them with curiosity. Somewhere a thumping bass line issuing from a car radio buzzed through the otherwise still afternoon air. He became aware of his own heartbeat and breathing and concentrated on keeping both slow and steady.

They got to the front porch of number 439 Willow Leaf Drive. Noah rang the doorbell, positioning himself just to the side of the door, next to a concrete planter full of purple petunias.

Franks was in a similar position on the opposite side. He saw movement through the door's diamond-shaped leaded glass window: a young man approached the door, stopped cold, and then darted away.

"He's running!"

"Go!" Noah said, gesturing Franks to take the right side of the house while he himself ran around to the left.

Franks cleared the first corner and ran straight on to the back yard. Before he got there, he heard a metal storm door slam shut, then the sound of shoes running on pavement. He cleared the side of the house just in time to see a tall, brown-haired young man running full speed toward the backyard of the house just behind his.

"Riverdale police!" Franks shouted. "Daniel Reed, stop right there!"

Noah sprinted across the yard to Franks' left, gaining on Reed. "2259 to Dispatch: suspect fled on foot, we are in pursuit," Noah reported, "heading west from 439 Willow Leaf Drive, cutting across adjacent properties. Suspect is wearing a black, long-sleeved shirt, blue jeans and gray and black shoes."

"Copy that, 2259. Alerting backup units."

Franks saw Reed look back at the pursuing detectives a few times before changing direction and heading to his right toward the house on the corner, whose back yard was surrounded by a six-foot tall wrought iron fence. Reed drew something from the waistband at his back and aimed it right at him. The shot went off just a fraction of a second before he shouted, "Gun!"

Franks had ducked down and zagged to the left. The bullet missed him. "Shots fired, shots fired!" he reported. "We've got a 417, armed suspect!" Avoiding the shot had cost him time and the distance between him and Reed widened to almost fifteen feet. Noah, however, was catching up to Reed like he'd been flung from a slingshot. Franks drew his gun and commanded, "Daniel Reed, drop your weapon and get down on the ground now!"

Reed replied by squeezing off one more wild shot, which caught Franks right in the chest. The impact knocked the breath from him and he dropped to the ground. "Frankie!" Noah shouted into the radio. Franks gasped for air, groping in the manicured grass for his weapon, which had fallen from his grasp as he hit the turf.

"Officer down, Officer down! Requesting medical assistance!" Noah shouted. "Hands in the air, Reed! Put the gun down!"

Franks looked up to see Reed stopped at the fence, hands wavering at his side. Noah was bearing down on him, gun trained right at Reed's chest. They were about a couple dozen feet away and he could hear them both clearly, even without the radio. "Stay back!" Reed shouted. "I can't go to jail! You don't understand!"

"Drop your weapon and get down on the ground now!" Noah was standing still now, lining up his shot in case he had to take it. Reed was still agitated, pacing in a tight formation.

Franks saw the dog before either Reed or Noah did, but couldn't get a breath to warn Noah. It barreled across the yard and right up to the fence, growling viciously, and lunged forward to grab Reed by the back of his shirt. He screamed and tried to turn to shoot the dog, but Noah brought him down with a shot to his leg instead. Reed fell, screaming, and the dog retreated to the safety of his doghouse, frightened off by the gunshot. "Suspect wounded, but in custody," Noah said.

Franks sucked in a painful breath and coughed, his head swimming. He closed his eyes a moment and groaned. "Dispatch, where are my medics?" Noah asked. A moment later, he was at Franks' side.

"Ambulance en route, 2259. ETA: one minute," the dispatcher answered.

"Frankie? Open your eyes, man. Talk to me – are you okay?"

Franks looked up and sucked in another breath. He rolled to his side and ran a hand over the vest. The bullet had lodged in the Kevlar, but there seemed to be something wrong with his chest. "Can't - breathe," he wheezed.

Noah made him lie flat on his back. "Just lie still," he cautioned, "you may have a couple of broken ribs." Noah knelt next to him. "Slow breaths, nice and easy." Franks did as directed, slowing his breathing, and winced at the pain. "That's it, just breathe. It's gonna hurt like hell, but you've got to keep breathing."

A patrol car and two ambulances screeched to a halt in the street just beyond the house with the fence, sirens blaring and lights flashing. The sirens all cut off and two uniformed officers and four paramedics rushed toward the scene. Within minutes Reed was secured in the back of one of the ambulances and Franks had recovered enough to stand and walk. The paramedics who checked him over – the same pair that treated Natalie Reynolds for her seizure – agreed the bullet had likely broken at least two ribs.

The petite blonde started him on an IV and gave him an injection of fentanyl for the pain while her partner hooked him up to a couple of different machines to monitor his heart. They wanted to make sure there was no internal damage as well, she said as she slipped an oxygen mask over his face, and insisted rather strongly that he let them take him to the ER. Noah hovered nearby.

"Go on with Reed," Franks told Noah. "I'll be right behind you."

Noah nodded and went over to the other ambulance. He got in and a paramedic shut the doors from inside. Franks leaned his head back and sighed. A moment later he realized he hadn't called his mother yet that day. The thought that he might've been seriously injured or killed without speaking to her one last time unsettled him. If it hadn't been for that vest...

He closed his eyes and thanked God for whomever invented Kevlar. And fentanyl. Especially fentanyl...

CHAPTER THIRTEEN

WHEN HE AND FRANKS arrived back at the precinct the next morning, they weren't there for more than half an hour before the next crisis struck. "Oh, crap," Noah groaned when he saw who was headed up the hall toward Ziehring's office.

"What?" Franks asked, wincing as he turned to look. He was going to be fine, the doctors said; no internal injuries, just three badly cracked ribs. Once Internal Affairs was through investigating the shooting, and Franks had paid a visit to his mother, he had announced that he was ready to go back to work.

"Jonathan Dalton is here."

"Oh, crap," Franks agreed.

Noah dug his cell phone out and dialed Ziehring's number. "Captain," he said when Ziehring answered, "Jonathan Dalton is here, in the station."

"I'll be right there. Where is he?"

"Coming right toward you." Noah started toward the Captain's office, with Franks in tow. "We're headed that way as well. Be right there." Noah hung up. "Mr. Dalton," he called loudly.

Dalton paused and turned toward Noah and Franks. "What? You two are still here? You should've been fired already."

"Mr. Dalton, what are you doing here?" Noah asked bluntly.

"I want my son. You've kept him here far too long, and he needs to come home, now." Dalton drew himself up to his full height, which wasn't all that impressive, and stared Noah in the eye.

"Mr. Dalton, are you harassing my detectives?" Ziehring asked from where he had come to stand behind him.

Dalton turned. "Me harassing them? Captain, I think you'll find it's the other way around. First, this one," he said, jabbing a finger at Noah, "watches my house all night, then they drag my son out of his bed and haul him down to – " he stopped speaking as he caught sight of Daniel Reed being escorted by a uniformed officer toward the men's room across from one of the interrogation rooms. The gunshot wound Noah had given him was not much more than a flesh wound, so he had been treated at the hospital and released into police custody.

Dalton's face went pale, then flushed a livid red. "You!" he yelled, loud enough everyone in the room went still. Ziehring put himself between Dalton and Reed, but Dalton kept trying to go around him to get to his illegitimate son. Reed was trembling.

"Get him out of here," Noah commanded the startled officer at Reed's side. The officer rushed the limping Reed on into the men's room.

"What has he done?" Dalton demanded. "Why is he here?"

"Mr. Dalton, we're in the middle of an active investigation here," Ziehring explained. "I can't divulge that information. Please, just go home and let my guys do their job."

Dalton seethed with anger. Noah, afraid that he might get a glimpse of the Marshals or Carmen, stepped forward and laid a hand on Dalton's shoulder, steering him toward the exit.

Dalton jerked away from Noah. "Get your hands off of me," he said in an eerily quiet voice. He straightened his suit jacket and marched toward the exit. As he passed it, his attention focused on the conference room, where Carmen sat with one of the Marshals. Noah groaned.

"He's seen her," he said to Ziehring before catching up with Dalton. He put himself in Dalton's line of sight. "Let me show you out, sir," he offered.

Dalton got right in Noah's face. "You won't look so smug when I'm done, Detective. No one messes with my family without reprisal."

"Threatening a police officer is not a very good idea, Mr. Dalton."

"Oh, that's not a threat. That's just how it is," he added with a glance at Carmen. With that he turned away and strode out the door, shoving it open so hard it slammed against the railing outside.

Once he was gone, Noah looked through the conference room window at Carmen. She sat stock still, her eyes wide with fright. Noah sighed and turned back to Franks. His partner's face reflected the dread Noah himself felt: Carmen and Daniel – and possibly Evan – were no longer safe.

CHAPTER FOURTEEN

NOAH AND FRANKS DROVE out to the Baileys' house around five o'clock that evening, after Daniel Reed had been officially processed into the system. Noah knew how important it was to tell them that they had found the guy that had killed their daughter in person. He was glad to see that the Reynolds' red SUV was parked behind the Baileys' blue one when they pulled up. Finding out the person who killed someone you love had been apprehended was always very emotional, and having friends present for support could only help.

Franks got out of the car with a groan, and Noah kept a close watch on him as they walked to the front door of the Baileys' modest two-story craftsman style home. The man should've been in bed, or at least resting at home. But he had insisted he was fit to return to duty and since the Internal Affairs officer who had interviewed them after the shooting had cleared them both, he refused to go home. Noah could tell he was in a lot of pain, but he wanted to be here just as much as Noah, and he had definitely earned the right.

He rang the doorbell and Mr. Bailey answered it a moment later. "Detectives," he said in surprise, opening the storm door for them, "please, come in." He stepped aside and let them in. "What is it? What's happened?" he asked as soon as the door closed behind them.

"Mr. Bailey, can we have a moment of you and your family's time?" Noah asked. "We have an update in the case we'd like to share with you all."

He nodded and swallowed hard. "Of course. Please, right this way." He led them through to the comfortable, inviting living room where Mrs. Bailey sat with the Reynoldses. They were all crying and sitting close, trying their best to comfort each other. The young Reynolds boy was the first to look up at their entrance. His eyes showed curiosity and respect and Noah gave him a grim nod.

"Honey," Mr. Bailey said, "the detectives are here. They have something to tell us."

All eyes turned to them. Noah and Franks crossed over to the middle of the room and faced the two families on which this crime had had such a tragic impact. "Detective Franks and I wanted to let you know that, earlier this afternoon, we located and apprehended the man responsible for Tasha's death."

Mr. Bailey sank to his knees next to the couch where his wife sat, sobbing. Mrs. Bailey took his hand and wept audibly. The Reynoldses gathered closer to them, hugging them and crying as well. Noah felt a lump forming in his throat and he knelt on the floor before Mrs. Bailey. He took her hand and said, "I know this won't bring her back, and I am so sorry that I can't do that for you, but at least you can know that this man won't ever be able to bring this kind of pain to any other family."

She squeezed his hand and gave him a small smile. "Thank you. Thank you both so much, I -" she began to cry again.

Franks stepped forward and put a hand on Mr. Bailey's slumped shoulders. He didn't say anything, just stood near him, offering his sympathy and comfort. Noah saw a tear gathering on his partner's eyelashes. He patted Mrs. Bailey's hands and stood.

"We'll keep you all informed as the case progresses, but you can always call us at any time if you need anything." He touched Franks' shoulder and, when Franks looked up, motioned toward the door.

Franks stood, but Mr. Bailey grabbed both his and Noah's hands. "God bless you both for what you've done for us."

Franks gave him a reassuring smile. "I only wish we could do more."

Noah and Franks left the families to their grief. They had just gotten to the car when Noah glanced back at the house. Natalie Reynolds and her brother had come to the door and were watching them through the glass storm door. The boy lifted a hand to wave, and then nudged his sister to get her to do the same. Noah returned their wave before getting into the car.

Franks and Noah stopped by a diner on the way back to the precinct. They ordered burgers and fries and drinks. Franks gave him a sidelong glance when Noah ordered ginger ale with his. "What?"

"Nothing," Franks answered with a disgusted sneer at the beverage. He shook his head. "So what happens now? I mean, the Marshals have upped their security on Carmen and Evan, and Daniel Reed will be in a separate, protective unit in prison until the trial is over. We have all the evidence in place to put him away for a good long while, so what do we do now?"

"Now we wait for the trial. You and I will be called to testify, the guys from the lab will present testimony about the evidence we collected and they processed. Mr. Crandall, Carmen and Evan will testify; Carmen more extensively than Evan, but he will have to appear. In the meantime, we work any other cases that come our way and make sure to check in with the Marshals from time to time to make sure our witnesses are safe."

"That's it?"

"Well you get to take it a little easier until your ribs heal up. But look on the bright side," he said with a smile.

"And what would that be?"

"Most cops go their whole career dreading the day they get shot and it never actually happens. You got shot in your first week here, so you can just relax now while the rest of us still have to stress about it every day."

Franks lifted his glass of Coke and said, "Well, then, here's to getting shot."

Noah clinked his glass against his partner's. "To getting shot and living to tell about it," he amended.

CHAPTER FIFTEEN

———

FOUR MONTHS LATER, the trial of Daniel Reed was over. He was indicted on vehicular manslaughter, leaving the scene of a fatal accident and aggravated assault on a police officer. His sentencing hearing was still weeks away, but he was no doubt going away for a long time. Noah and Franks had given their testimony, along with Carmen and Mr. Crandall, the witness to Tasha's death.

The judge had been made aware of Daniel Reed's paternity and the fact that he had tried to pass himself off as Evan Dalton in private sessions in his chambers prior to any proceedings and had ruled that, while the evidence must be presented to the jury, the public must be kept ignorant for fear of putting Reed's and Carmen's lives in danger. The entire proceedings were kept closed to the public and press, and the jurors were bound by strict non-disclosure orders.

The trial came and went without the most people even knowing about it. Carmen had returned to her home, promising Franks she would soon relocate and get into another line of work. Evan Dalton moved across the country, leaving contact information with the precinct, but no one else.

Noah and Franks moved on to other cases. They spent most of their days chasing up leads and following up with witnesses or checking in with the lab. Franks – or Frankie, as most people called him now – had settled in well and was gaining popularity with some of the other detectives. That included Noah, who had grown to respect his new partner. He even accompanied Franks on visits to his mother in the hospital now and then and had found Mrs. Franks to be a loving, warm and intelligent woman. He saw the love that the two had for each other and felt that old recurring pang of grief and jealousy trying to rear its head. Losing his parents so young had left scars so deep he feared they would never heal; yet he was glad for Franks and his mother. Her time was running shorter, and the more love she experienced in this world, the easier it would be for her son to accept her passing into the next.

It happened the day Noah and Franks closed a missing person case they had been working for over two months. They were in the middle of a celebratory lunch when Franks' cell phone rang. Noah knew immediately what had happened by the look on his partner's face.

Franks' breathing increased and tears flooded his eyes. "I'll be right there," he told the caller before hanging up. He looked up at Noah. "I've gotta go," he said, dazed.

Noah dug out enough money to cover their meals and tossed it onto the table. "Give me the keys," he said, holding out a hand.

Minutes later Noah pulled up outside the hospital. Franks jumped out almost before the car was stopped and ran into the building. Noah finished parking and followed him inside. He waited in the hall while his partner went into the room where his mother's body lay. The doctor was with her and explained what had happened in comforting tones. Franks slumped into the chair by her bed, reaching his hand to cover her small frail one. He bowed his head and sobbed brokenly.

The doctor quietly took his leave, pausing to give Noah a sad smile. "It's good you're here, Detective Harkham," he said. "He's going to need all the friends he can get right now."

Noah nodded and slipped into the room. He sat in the other chair, the one in which he had often sat while visiting with Mrs. Franks, and put a hand on Franks' back. Mrs. Franks looked so small compared to the way she had looked just that morning, yet she had a peaceful expression on her face.

Tears fell from Noah's eyes as well. He grieved for both his partner's loss and his own. Mrs. Franks had welcomed him warmly, treating him almost as her own, and he knew he would miss her greatly. He sat in silence with Franks until the doctors and nurses came back for her.

The following Saturday was warm and sunny, as if oblivious to the pain so many felt as they said goodbye to a wonderful mother, sister and friend. The funeral service had been beautiful and several of his colleagues had come to support Franks in his grief. When it was all over and everyone who had come to pay their respects had left the cemetery, Franks and Noah paid a visit to Tasha Bailey's grave.

The Bailey's had been there recently; a small bouquet of daisies had been left in the vase attached to the gravestone. Franks added a small bunch of carnations as well.

"Will it ever get any easier?" Franks asked as they got back to his car.

Noah swallowed thickly. "Eventually," he answered. "But it takes time."

Franks nodded slowly, emotion obviously robbing him of his voice momentarily. "How did you do it? How did you deal with it?"

Noah started the car and drove up the meandering path through the cemetery. "I still deal with it, every day, to some degree. The ones you love never really leave you, even if they are taken from you. But eventually the pain of losing them gets sort of drowned out by all the good memories." He drove back to Franks' apartment, and they spent the rest of the day swapping stories about their parents. Noah also told Franks all about Rob Meares, and made sure to mention how much alike he thought the two were.

TWO WEEKS LATER, ZIEHRING called them into his office. They sat across from their captain and received the news they had begun to think would never come: the papers had gotten wind of the fact that Daniel Reed was Jonathan Dalton's son and had run the story about his arrest for Tasha Bailey's murder.

Before they could find Carmen to take her into protective custody, her body was found behind a Dumpster, two days after the story ran. Her death was ruled an accidental drug overdose. Evan Dalton contacted them a few days after that to say that he was in the hospital, after fighting off a pair of men in ski masks who had tried to force him into a van. He went into the WITSEC program just days afterward, shedding the Dalton name forever.

While nothing was ever found to tie Jonathan Dalton to either crime, Noah and Franks kept Carmen's case open, and her photo graced Franks' desk from that day forward.

Don't miss out!

Visit the website below and you can sign up to receive emails whenever J.I. O'Neal publishes a new book. There's no charge and no obligation.

https://books2read.com/r/B-A-MNEF-LHZP

BOOKS 2 READ

Connecting independent readers to independent writers.

Did you love *Impact: A Riverdale PD Series Prequel*? Then you should read *Indiscriminate: 5th Anniversary Revised Edition*[1] by J.I. O'Neal!

[2]

He paused in the shadows of a darkened shop to glance once more at the historic brick building. A symbol of peace of mind. It was robbed of that peace now, and he was the thief.

In August, 2013, Detective Sergeant Noah Harkham's stellar career came to a violent end when devastating injuries rendered him deaf and blind on his left side. Now, nine months later, a string of attacks on rescue personnel has thrown the city of Riverdale into a panic.

When it becomes apparent that this case has its origin in one Noah worked with his former partner and best friend, Detective Alan Franks, Noah is determined to help put an end to the chaos.

---

1. https://books2read.com/u/bwWNR9

2. https://books2read.com/u/bwWNR9

Noah must overcome his disabilities to aid in the manhunt for the city's most wanted criminal – even as the attacker draws closer to those Noah and Franks hold dear.

Also by J.I. O'Neal

Riverdale PD Series
Impact: A Riverdale PD Series Prequel
Indiscriminate: 5th Anniversary Revised Edition
Time of Death

Stell-Ore War
The Crew of Cartage 15
Stell-Ore Justice